'You made it c
that you don't
makes no differ
you.'

Too late she realised that she had nowhere to go. Lucas had backed her up against the bed, the edge of which fitted nicely behind her knees. If he moved only a fraction, she would fall. She shivered as she pictured all too vividly what might come next.

'Just a kiss, Emily,' he whispered. 'As thanks for the flowers, or goodnight, or whatever reason suits you best—'

At the first touch of his lips on hers, Emily's legs buckled. She sat abruptly on the bed, and Lucas fell to his knees beside her, hauling her against his chest to kiss her with such force and hunger she yielded to him, powerless to control her response.

'You see what you reduce me to?' he demanded roughly, raising his head a fraction. 'Does it give you a kick to see me on my knees?'

Catherine George was born in Wales, and early on developed a passion for reading which eventually fuelled her compulsion to write. Marriage to an engineer led to nine years in Brazil, but on his later travels the education of her son and daughter kept her in the UK. And instead of constant reading to pass her lonely evenings she began to write the first of her romantic novels. When not writing and reading she loves to cook, listen to opera, browse in antique shops and walk the Labrador.

Recent titles by the same author:

SARAH'S SECRET
SWEET SURRENDER

CITY
CINDERELLA

BY
CATHERINE GEORGE

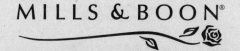

MILLS & BOON®

*MILLS & BOON and MILLS & BOON with the Rose Device
are registered trademarks of the publisher.*

*First published in Great Britain 2003
Harlequin Mills & Boon Limited,
Eton House, 18-24 Paradise Road, Richmond, Surrey TW9 1SR*

© Catherine George 2003

ISBN 0 263 83224 4

*Set in Times Roman 10½ on 12 pt.
01-0403-46631*

*Printed and bound in Spain
by Litografía Rosés, S.A., Barcelona*

CHAPTER ONE

THE wind from the Thames came whistling up the cobbled street as he paid off the taxi. Aching in every bone, he hurried into the building and leaned against the wall in the lift, cursing the virus that had finally caught up with him. On the top floor he heaved himself upright when the doors opened, and with a groan of relief at the prospect of warmth let himself into the loft apartment he called home. He shrugged off his overcoat, dumped his briefcase on the pile of mail on the military chest in the hall, and, desperate for hot coffee with a slug of Scotch in it, opened the kitchen door. And stood rooted to the spot.

The kitchen's stainless steel and granite was immaculate, as expected. But it was occupied. A young woman he'd never seen in his life sat on one of the retro-style stools at his breakfast bar, tapping away at a laptop, her concentration so intense she had no idea he was there.

Before he could demand an explanation his sudden, hacking cough brought the stranger's head swivelling round, her eyes wide in utter dismay as she slid to her feet to face him.

'Mr Tennent?' she said at last, in a surprisingly deep, husky voice for someone only an inch or so over five feet. 'I do apologise. This is the very first time, I swear.'

Lucas Tennent remained standing in the doorway, staring at her blankly, his thought processes blunted by the dull pounding in his head. 'The first time for what? Who the devil are you?'

'I'm your cleaner.'

He blinked. 'My *cleaner*?'

She nodded, flushing. 'Thank you for the cheque you left for me today—unless you'd like it back now.'

'Why the hell should I want it back?' he said irritably, grappling with the fact that this was the E Warner who kept his flat in mint condition. Not elderly and aproned, but young, in jeans and skimpy sweatshirt, with soot-black curling hair skewered up in an untidy knot.

'Mr Tennent,' she said after a moment, eyeing him closely. 'You don't look at all well.'

'I feel bloody awful,' he snapped. 'But keep to the point. Explain about the laptop.'

'I was using my batteries, not your electricity,' she said defensively.

'My sole interest, of course,' he said with blighting sarcasm. 'Tell me what you were doing.'

Her jaw set. 'I'd rather not do that.'

'Tell me just the same,' he said relentlessly.

'Nothing criminal, Mr Tennent,' she said with hauteur. 'I'm—doing a correspondence course.'

'So where do you normally work on it?'

'In my room. But this week it's half-term. At the moment peace and quiet are in short supply where I live. So I did some work here today. But only after I finished your cleaning,' she assured him.

'Sorry I came home early to spoil your fun—' he began, the rest of his words engulfed in a sudden spasm of coughing. To his surprise, he was gently taken by the arm and led towards the breakfast bar.

'Sit there for a moment, Mr Tennent,' she said with sympathy. 'Do you have any medication?'

He shook his head, gasping for breath as he subsided

on a stool. 'No. I just need coffee. Make me some and I'll double your money.'

She gave him a withering look and turned on her heel, presenting a back view rigid with offence while she dealt with the machine guaranteed to turn beans into coffee at top speed. Lucas sat silent, chin on hands, diverted from the thumping in his head by the sight of E Warner tugging her sweatshirt down to cover an inch of bare midriff as she put her laptop to sleep and closed it before pouring the coffee.

'When I came in I thought I was hallucinating, Ms Warner,' he remarked eventually, as the scent of his best Blue Mountain filled the air. 'But a laptop seemed an unlikely accessory for housebreaking.' He took a relishing gulp of the strong, steaming liquid she set in front of him. 'Thank you. I think you just saved my life.'

She shook her head, frowning. 'Not really, Mr Tennent. You should be in bed.'

'I will be shortly.' He raised an eyebrow. 'Aren't you having any coffee?'

Her smile activated a dimple near the corner of her mouth. Which was a very enticing feature, he noticed—unpainted, full-lipped, and eminently kissable. The curves outlined by the sweatshirt were equally enticing... And the fever was obviously affecting his brain, he thought in swift disgust, hoping she couldn't read his mind.

'It seemed best to wait until invited,' she said ruefully.

Lucas nodded, then winced when the movement made his headache worse. 'Do please join me, Ms Warner,' he said formally. 'Or are you Mrs?'

'Miss.'

'What does the E stand for?'

'Emily.' She eyed him, frowning. 'Mr Tennent, do you mind if I touch your forehead?'

'Not at all.' He submitted to a cool hand laid briefly on his brow, and sat back. 'Diagnosis?'

'High temperature. You've got flu, hopefully.'

'Hopefully?'

'I meant rather than anything worse.' She hesitated, then bent to search in a backpack on the floor and came up with a packet of paracetamol. 'Will you take these? Two now and two tonight, and drink plenty of fluids.'

He stared at her in surprise. 'That's very kind of you, Emily, or do you prefer Ms Warner?'

'You pay my wages, Mr Tennent. Your choice.' She looked at her watch, then stowed her laptop in the backpack. 'I won't have any coffee, thank you. Time I was off. I'm taking the twins to the cinema.'

His eyebrows rose. 'Twins?'

'The children on half-term. Their father's my landlord, and I'm taking them off his hands for a couple of hours,' she explained. 'I did your shopping on the way in, so there's plenty of orange juice and fruit. Goodbye, Mr Tennent. I'll be in on Monday as usual.' She eyed him with concern. 'Is there someone who can look after you?'

'I wouldn't ask my worst enemy to risk this blasted bug. Which you could be doing right now,' he added suddenly.

Her shake of the head dislodged another hank of hair. 'I've already had flu this winter.'

'What did you do to get over it?'

'Went home to my parents to be cosseted.'

'My mother's asthmatic, so that's out of the question.' He shrugged. 'And otherwise I prefer to wallow alone in my misery.'

She pulled on her jacket and thrust her arms through the straps of her backpack. 'There's no point in calling a doctor if it's flu, of course. Not unless you develop something else, like bronchitis. But please take the pills—eight a day max—and drink lots of water. A good thing it's Friday, Mr Tennent. You'll have the weekend to get over it.'

'If I live that long,' he said morosely, and saw her to the door.

'Mr Tennent,' she said diffidently as he opened it.

'Yes?'

'I'm sorry.'

His bloodshot eyes narrowed to an unsettling gleam. 'Because I feel like death, or because you were caught in the act?'

Her chin lifted. 'Both. Please accept the coffee-making for free by way of recompense,' she added, and stepped into the lift.

Her mind occupied with Lucas Tennent, for once Emily Warner had no eyes for the view of the Thames as she crossed Tower Bridge. Up to now, the man she worked for had just been one of her four employers. He left a cheque every week for her wages, and owned a flat she'd give her eye-teeth to live in. But now she could put a face and body to the name the situation was different. He'd given her the shock of her life by catching her redhanded, of course. But her first startled glimpse of Lucas Tennent was rubber-stamped on her brain, partly because he'd looked so ghastly she'd been afraid he was about to pass out on her.

Oblivious of traffic noise and passers-by, Emily hurried back to Spitalfields, her mind busy with the physical details of the employer she'd never actually met before.

There were no photographs of him in his apartment, but because he did something in the banking world she'd visualised brains as well as brawn. In the flesh, Lucas Tennent was well over six feet tall, his windblown hair black as her own, possibly eyes to match, when they weren't too bloodshot to tell. His intelligence was self-evident, but it came combined with dark, smouldering good looks undiminished by even his current deathly pallor. And his Savile Row suit was no disguise for the musculature she would have expected, since it was part of her job to dust the rowing machine and treadmill up in the gallery. Emily sighed enviously. All that space for just one man. If she lived there she could work on her laptop to her heart's content under the gallery's pitched glass roof, which not only boasted sunblinds controlled electronically by temperature, but led on to a roof terrace overlooking the Thames. Perfect. And in total contrast to her solitary room on the second floor of a house owned by one of her brother's friends.

But it was a pretty room, and she was lucky to have it, she reminded herself as she reached the familiar cobbled street. Built originally for refugee Huguenot silk weavers in the seventeen hundreds, most of the houses in this part of Spitalfields had been painstakingly restored, including the one owned by her landlord. Nat Sedley was an architect with a London firm and a home in the Cotswolds. Originally he had bought the house in Spitalfields as a city base. But he now lived in it permanently, with only his two tenants for company, while his children remained with his estranged wife in the house in the country.

When Emily reached the railings which flanked the front door it flew open to reveal two excited six-year-olds lying in wait in the hall, ready and raring to go.

'They've been dressed for ages,' said their father, grinning in apology. 'I warned them you might want tea first but it fell on deaf ears.'

'I'll just dump my things and we're away,' Emily assured them, rewarded at once by beams from two faces so unalike it was hard to believe that Thomas and Lucy were brother and sister, let alone twins.

'I'll have supper waiting when you get back,' said Nat, as he saw them into a taxi. 'Now be good, you two, and maybe we can coax Emily to share it with us.'

By the time she'd brought the jubilant twins back to Spitalfields Nat Sedley had the promised supper waiting, and Emily not only enjoyed a family meal, but surrendered to pleas to stay afterwards until the twins were ready for bed.

'Thanks a lot, Em,' said Nat gratefully, as she made for the stairs later. 'You're a life-saver.'

She chuckled. 'That's the second time I've heard that today.'

Nat demanded details, amused when he heard she'd been caught red-handed at her laptop. 'But I'm sorry you were driven out to find quiet to work. I should have put your room out of bounds to the twins from the first. By way of a peace offering, fancy coming down later this evening for a drink?'

She smiled. 'Thanks, I'd like that very much.'

In the quiet of her room, Emily collapsed into a chair, suddenly weary. The outing with the twins had been great fun, but after a morning spent cleaning two apartments, followed by a couple of hours' solid slog on her laptop, the confrontation with Lucas Tennent had rather knocked the stuffing out of her. He'd had every right to sack her on the spot, too, which would have done serious damage to her finances. Lucky for her he'd been feeling

so rough, otherwise he might not have taken her trespass
nearly so well. She'd felt like Goldilocks caught by the
bear. Emily chuckled. Wrong hair, wrong fairy tale.
There were no fireplaces in Lucas Tennent's flat, but her
role was Cinderella just the same. And she'd done no
harm, other than just being there in his kitchen, where
she wasn't supposed to be on a Friday afternoon.

But from now on her activities in Mr Lucas Tennent's
flat would be restricted to the cleaning duties he paid
her for. Emily frowned, wondering how he was feeling.
He'd looked so ill she'd been a bit reluctant to leave him
to fend for himself. Which was nonsense. If she hadn't
stayed on for an extra hour or two she wouldn't have
met him, nor known about his flu.

Emily took a reviving shower, dried her hair and
treated her hands and face to some extra care, grateful
to Nat for asking her down for a drink. Much as she
despised herself for it, Friday evenings were still hard to
get used to on her own. And to add to her pleasure, when
she arrived in Nat's small, panelled drawing-room her
fellow tenant, Mark Cooper, gave her a hug and shep-
herded her to the sofa to join his girlfriend, Bryony
Talbot.

'Hi, Emily.' Bryony patted the place beside her.
'Come and sit down. Are you exhausted? Nat said
you've been entertaining the twins.'

'And enjoying it. Evening all. How are you feeling
now, Mark?' asked Emily. 'Recovered from your cold?'

He nodded, smiling smugly. 'Bryony kissed me better.'

Nat shook his head as he handed Emily a glass of
wine. 'His own private nurse, lucky beggar.'

'But my medical skills don't come cheap,' said

Bryony promptly. 'He's buying me a *very* expensive dinner tomorrow night.'

Emily chuckled. 'Demand Claridges, at the very least.'

Mark winked at her. 'Flash your dimple at me like that, Emily, and I'll bring you back a doggy bag.'

'Gee, thanks!'

'Lots of strange bugs about where I earn my crust, though,' he commented, squeezing between his beloved and Emily on the sofa. 'Move up, you two.'

'Can't you sit on a chair?' complained Bryony affectionately.

'Much more fun like this, darling.'

Emily felt a stab of concern at Mark's mention of bugs. But Lucas Tennent was big enough and old enough to look after himself. And he could call on professional medical help if he became really ill; a thought which allowed her to relax in the stimulating company of people she liked very much. Mark rented the floor below hers in Nat's house, and along with Bryony had been a good friend when Emily, in urgent need of somewhere in London to live, had taken Nat up on his offer of a room. With two homes to keep up, her landlord insisted he could do with all the extra money he could get. Emily had scoffed at his idea of rent, which was ridiculously low for London. But Nat was a close friend of her brother, Andrew, and remained adamant. In the end she had pocketed the pride she couldn't afford, grateful for his help and generosity.

After a place to live, a new job had been the next priority on the agenda. When Emily moved into the room in Nat's house he had been trying for some time to find a suitable replacement for his cleaner, who wanted to retire. Because the elegant house was very old, and correspondingly fragile, he needed someone who would treat it with the care and respect it deserved. But when Emily proposed herself as substitute, at the same rate of pay, Nat thought she was joking at first. At last, when he realised she was in deadly earnest, he agreed with enthusiasm, and the moment Mark heard about it he begged Emily to take on his rooms as well. When it became obvious that Emily actually enjoyed cleaning, Nat asked permission to recommend her to one of his married female colleagues who'd just acquired a new flat in Bermondsey. The added job proved such a happy arrangement that Liz Donaldson soon suggested Emily kill two birds with one stone and also take on a friend's loft apartment in the converted warehouse across the street. And so what had been intended as a stop-gap before finding another secretarial job suddenly snowballed into a whole new career.

Emily's parents disapproved strongly, and friends thought she was raving mad. But in secret she was working to plan. The new job left her mind and imagination free to function separately from her busy, careful hands, and at the same time paid enough to provide financial backing while she tried her hand at writing a novel. Taken on the hop, she'd had to fib to Lucas Tennent, because not even her nearest and dearest had any idea what she was really up to in her spare time.

The plot of her novel was already mapped out, with some of the main characters automatically cast: villain and wicked witch no problem at all. But she'd had difficulty in conjuring up a charismatic central male. Nat was outrageously handsome, and Mark boyish-faced and charming. But, despite covert observation of both men as a possible role model, her hero had stubbornly refused to come to life. Then Lucas Tennent had caught her *in flagrante* with her laptop today, and wham, her main character had materialised right before her startled, guilty eyes.

After a couple of hours, much as she was enjoying herself in such convivial company, Emily resisted pleas to stay longer and went up early to her room. She sat down at her desk, booted up the laptop, and set to work on her novel. By the time she went to bed she felt tired, but very pleased with herself. Adding Lucas Tennent's physical assets to the previously bare bones of her central male character had provided her with exactly the charismatic hero she needed for her plot.

The moment Emily was dressed next morning the twins came knocking on her door. 'Hi, you two,' she said affectionately.

'Dad said we mustn't bother you if you're busy,' said Thomas in one breath, then smiled cajolingly. 'But please come down for coffee. We've got to go after lunch.'

'We'll miss you,' said Lucy, giving Emily a hug.

'But you'll be seeing Mummy today, sweetheart, so you won't need me. I bet she's missed you a lot,' said Emily, deliberately cheerful. 'Give her my love.'

Lucy's big blue eyes filled with tears. 'Emily, will *you* ask Mummy to be friends with Daddy again?'

'You can't ask Emily to do that!' said her twin gruffly.

Emily went downstairs with the children, wishing she *could* do something to help. But the Sedleys' private affairs were none of her business. She'd known them both a long time, it was true, but had no idea what sin Nat had committed that Thea found impossible to forgive. Nor did she want to know. Sorting out her own personal life was more than enough.

Emily enjoyed a lively half-hour with the twins, but

when they were settled in front of Saturday morning television Nat beckoned her into his kitchen and shut the door.

'Why has Lucy been crying?'

Emily looked at him squarely. 'She wanted me to ask Thea to be friends with you again, and Tom told her that wasn't on.'

His handsome face went blank. 'Are you going to do that?'

'Do you want me to?'

Nat was silent for a moment, then gave her a smile just like his son's. 'If I thought it would do any good, yes. But it won't.' He shivered a little. 'Forget it, love. Don't get involved.'

Emily eyed him with suspicion. 'Are you all right, Nat? Not coming down with something, too, are you?'

'Too?'

'Like Mark,' she said hastily.

He shook his head. 'I'm just dandy, other than taking my children back to the love of my life, who won't let me over the doorstep.' He forced a smile. 'You've had enough upset in your life lately without worrying about me, Emily. Enjoy your weekend.'

But before getting ready to go out Emily gave in to her prodding conscience and rang Lucas Tennent, who growled a response so hoarse it was obvious he was worse than the day before.

'Good morning,' she said briskly, 'this is Emily Warner.'

'*Who?*'

She bristled. 'Your cleaner, Mr Tennent. I wondered how you were feeling today.'

'Oh, right.' There was a pause. 'Actually, I feel bloody awful.'

'Have you eaten anything?'

A spasm of coughing blasted her ear before he spoke again. 'No,' he rasped. 'Not hungry.'

'Is your temperature still high?'

'Probably.' He gulped audibly. 'Oh, *hell*—'

Emily seethed for a moment after he disconnected, then told herself it was idiotic to feel offended. Even more so to worry about a perfect stranger. Especially one who couldn't remember who she was.

Mindful of Ginny, who always looked effortlessly right, Emily took time over her appearance, then went downstairs for a last hug from the twins before she set off for Knightsbridge to meet her friend.

'I say, darling, you look rather gorgeous today,' exclaimed Ginny Hart, when Emily joined her in the Harvey Nichols coffee shop.

'I like the "today" bit,' chuckled Emily, shedding the amber wool coat bought in the days when she still had a high-salary job. 'I try my best every day.'

'A bargain, that coat—matches your eyes,' commented Ginny, and eyed the clinging black knit dress with approval. 'Don't tell me you wear that kind of thing to scrub floors!'

'I don't scrub floors. My clients provide labour-saving devices. Like mops.'

Ginny sniffed. 'The tyrant who cleans for us demands extraordinary things. A new three-inch paintbrush to dust the skirtings, would you believe?'

Saturday morning coffee had been a treat enjoyed together in the days of flat-sharing, and a ritual kept to whenever possible since, despite marriage for Ginny and a relationship of a less binding nature for Emily.

'So what's new?' asked Ginny, after their order arrived.

'I met the man I clean for at last,' said Emily, raising her voice slightly.

'The mystery man on the top floor?' said Ginny, and bent her blonde head nearer. 'What's he like? Tall, dark and gorgeous?'

'Yes,' said Emily, giggling when Ginny's jaw dropped.

'*Really?* Not sinister after all, then. Frankly, I always thought it a bit iffy that he took you on without an interview.'

'You know perfectly well he took me on trust because Liz Donaldson gave me such a glowing reference.'

'As well she might,' Ginny frowned. 'But you're not going to do this kind of thing forever, surely?'

'Of course not. But for the time being I'm enjoying it. I work at my own speed in very pleasant surroundings. Especially Lucas Tennent's loft.' Emily looked her friend in the eye. 'Right now the work is good therapy for me.'

Ginny sniffed. 'And at least you're being paid to do it, unlike—' She held up a hand. 'All right, I'll shut up. Tell me about this sexy banker, then, now you've finally met up with him.'

Emily described the meeting in graphic detail, winning peals of laughter from her friend. 'Actually, he was very nice about it, Ginny. I can't help thinking about him, to be honest.'

'Because he's gorgeous?'

'*No*—because the poor man's ill with no one to look after him.'

Ginny ordered more coffee, then turned to Emily with a militant light in her eye. 'You say this man's no turn-

off in the looks department, probably earns pots of
money, and lives in a loft apartment overlooking the
Thames. Come *on*, Em! There must be hordes of females
panting to mop his fevered brow.'

'Bound to be. But apparently he'd rather wallow in
misery alone.' Emily stirred her fresh coffee, frowning.
'Which he'll have to all weekend. I'm not due at his
place again until Monday morning.'

'Good. See you keep it that way.' Ginny reached to
touch Emily's hand. 'You're just beginning to get your
life back together, so for pity's sake stop worrying about
a man you hardly know.'

To change the subject Emily suggested some leisurely
window shopping rather than spending another afternoon
in the cinema, and as usual the time flew in company
with Ginny, with no opportunity for introspection. But
later, during the journey on the Tube and the walk to
Nat's house, no matter how hard she tried to block him
out, Emily couldn't help worrying about Lucas Tennent.

The feeling persisted during the evening. Emily
worked for a while on her laptop, but because she'd
based her main male character on Lucas Tennent the
procedure was a washout as a way to stop thinking about
him. At one point she even picked up the phone to ring
him. But in the end she put it back without dialling and
settled down to work instead. And eventually achieved
such fierce concentration it was long after midnight before she closed the laptop and fell into bed.

Emily woke with a start next morning, hoping Lucas
Tennent hadn't developed pneumonia in the night just
because she hadn't troubled to check. And when he answered the phone she felt totally justified, because he
sounded even worse than the time before. Before she

could even ask how he was, he gasped something incoherent and rang off.

A couple of hours later, feeling like Red Riding Hood off to visit the wolf, Emily turned down the cobbled street towards Lucas Tennent's building, bag of shopping in hand. Cursing the nagging conscience which had driven her there, she rang his bell first then unlocked the door.

'It's Emily Warner, Mr Tennent,' she called. 'Your cleaner. May I come in?'

There was silence for so long Emily was sure he must be lying unconscious somewhere. But eventually Lucas Tennent materialised in the doorway to his bedroom. He'd looked ill enough at their first encounter, but now he looked ghastly, his ashen pallor accentuated by streaks of unhealthy colour along his cheekbones. His bloodshot eyes were underscored by marks like bruises, his jaw black with stubble, and his tousled hair lank with sweat.

'What the hell are you doing here?' he grated through chattering teeth, and wrapped his dressing-gown closer.

Emily flushed. 'You sounded so ill I was worried. I thought you might need—'

'For God's sake go away. I don't need anything—' He gave a frantic gulp and raced off, kicking the bedroom door shut behind him.

Emily glared at it, incensed. So much for her Good Samaritan act. Seething, she slapped the newspaper down on the chest, added a carton of fresh milk, and was halfway through the door with the rest of her unwanted shopping when a hoarse, repentant voice halted her.

'Miss Warner—Emily. I was bloody rude. My apologies.'

She turned to look at him. 'Accepted,' she said coldly. 'Goodbye.'

'Don't go for a minute. Please.' He leaned in the bedroom doorway, shivering. 'Though Lord knows you should run like hell, in case you catch this hellish bug. Sorry I snapped.' His mouth twisted in distaste. 'I took off because I had to throw up again.'

Emily thawed slightly and closed the door. 'In that case please get back into bed.'

'Not a very tempting prospect right now.'

'Did you perspire much overnight?'

His mouth twisted in distaste. 'Could we talk about something else?'

She hesitated, then took the plunge. 'Look, Mr Tennent, why don't you have a hot shower while I change your bed?'

He looked appalled. 'I can't possibly let you do that!'

'Why not? I would have done it tomorrow, anyway. It's one of the things you pay me for.' She smiled encouragingly. 'You'll feel much better afterwards—but don't get your hair wet.'

He eyed her in brooding indecision for a moment, then shrugged, went into his bedroom, took a T-shirt and boxers from a drawer, and shut himself in his bathroom. Emily stripped the crumpled linen from the bed, replaced it with fresh, fetched more pillows from the spare room, and did some quick tidying up. When Lucas emerged his face was still haggard, but it was free of stubble and he'd run a comb through his hair.

When Emily turned back the quilt invitingly Lucas shed his dressing gown and slid into bed to lean back against the stacked pillows with a heartfelt sigh of relief.

'Thank you so much,' he said formally.

She smiled in acknowledgement. 'I'll dispose of this lot, then I'll make you something to eat.'

'Please—no food!' he said with a shudder, eyes closed.

'Just some toast,' she coaxed, in the tone she used with the twins. 'How many pills have you taken today?'

He opened a morose eye. 'None. With my present problem it seemed a bit pointless.'

'If you eat something you'll be able to keep them down.'

'I doubt it,' he said despondently.

In the kitchen Emily made tea, toasted a slice of bread she'd brought, scraped a minimum of butter on it, cut it in triangles, then put plate and beaker on a tray and took it into the master bedroom.

'If you make friends with the toast I could scramble some eggs,' she offered.

'I'm not up to that,' he said with a shudder. He bit into the toast and chewed slowly, then took a second piece and ate it more quickly.

'Steady,' warned Emily. 'Not too fast.'

'It's my first sustenance for days!' But he ate the rest with more care. 'Toast never tasted so good,' he informed her, then inspected the steaming contents of the mug with suspicion. 'What's this?'

'Weak tea—kinder to your digestion than coffee,' she said firmly, and took two paracetamol tablets from the packet on his bedside table. 'Take these with it, and I'll make you some coffee later.'

Lucas swallowed the tablets obediently, then sipped the tea, frowning at her over the mug. 'You know, Miss Warner, this is extraordinarily good of you, but why are you here? You must have better things to do with your time on a Sunday?'

She shrugged. 'I had my very first dose of flu fairly recently, so I can appreciate how ghastly you feel. But I had my mother to look after me. I couldn't help feeling worried about you here on your own.'

He shook his head in wonder. 'You're pretty amazing to worry about a complete stranger. But now you are here, there is something you can do for me.'

'Certainly. What is it?'

'Indulge my curiosity. What made someone like you take to cleaning as a career?'

'Someone like me?' she said, raising an eyebrow.

'I'm damned sure you haven't always been a cleaner, so why do you do it?'

'I enjoy it,' she said simply.

'Fair enough.' He put the empty cup down and slid further under the covers. 'But what did you do before that?'

'Office work.' She got up. 'Right. I'll take those things. Try to sleep if you can. I'll stay for a while to see how you get on, then I must get back.'

'No laptop today?'

'Certainly not. Friday was a one-off, Mr Tennent.' She picked up the tray. 'Try to sleep.'

'Thanks, I will,' he murmured drowsily. 'What can I do for you in return?'

'Get better, please.'

Back in the kitchen Emily emptied the carton of soup she'd bought into a mug and put it in the microwave. She left the loaf in a prominent place on a board, placed the breadknife beside it and a dish of butter close at hand, then made herself some tea and sat on one of the smart stools at the bar, yawning. The late night was catching up on her. From now on, definitely no more writing after midnight.

She wrote instructions on the memo pad about the
food she'd left ready, and after a moment's hesitation
added her new, unlisted phone number. She tiptoed in
with her note to find that Lucas Tennent, obviously feeling the effect of his disturbed nights, was out for the
count. But he looked a lot better than the wild-eyed ap-
parition of earlier on.

The house in Spitalfields was ablaze with lights in
Nat's ground-floor section when Emily got back. Not
brave enough to ask how things had gone with the trip
to Chastlecombe, she let herself in and toiled up the two
flights of steep stairs to her room, then put on speed
when she heard her phone ringing. She unlocked her
door and made a dash across the room, worried it was
Lucas feeling worse. Then she stopped dead, every
hackle erect, when a different, all too familiar voice began leaving a message.

'Pick up, Emily. I know you're there. We need to talk.
Pick *up*.' There was a pause, then a soft chuckle. 'Don't
be childish. Ring me.'

CHAPTER TWO

EMILY glared at the machine. The mere sound of Miles Denny's voice still tied her stomach in knots. But with cold animosity now. Once upon a time she'd been attracted to the sexy drawl he cultivated. Just as, according to Miles, her own husky voice had been an instant turn-on for him. But that had been in the beginning when he'd been moving heaven and earth to get her to live with him. Emily clenched her fists. With hindsight she found it hard to believe she could have been such a fool.

She had been working in a firm of commercial property consultants when Miles joined the company, and almost from the day they met he'd pursued her relentlessly. Firmly against inter-office relationships, Emily had held him off at first. But his persistence had been flattering, she'd been lonely without Ginny, and eventually, after wearing her down with months of persuasion, he'd won. But, once they were actually sharing a home, Miles' contribution to the running of it was minimal. In the evenings, while Emily cooked their meal and dealt with housework and laundry, he spent his time on the sofa, recharging his batteries in front of the television. Her only break had been on Friday nights, when Miles took her out for a meal.

How could she have been so stupid? she thought in disgust. Living together had soon shown her how little they had in common, and when Miles had taken to spending regular time with male friends after work Emily had thoroughly enjoyed the evenings with no dinner to cook and the television firmly turned off. Early to bed with a book had meant she was always asleep, or pretending to be, by the time Miles came home.

When it had become obvious that a good night's sleep was infinitely preferable to the lovemaking she'd found so disappointing with Miles, Emily had known it was time to move on. Deciding to tell him straight away, she'd waited up until he got home from one of his men-only evenings. And discovered why Miles had always been so meticulous about showering before sharing their bed. He'd reeked of musky, alien perfume and other scents Emily had identified with furious distaste.

The phone rang, bringing her back to the present with a bump. She tensed, eyeing the phone belligerently, but this time the message was from Lucas Tennent.

Emily seized the receiver. 'I'm here,' she said breathlessly. 'Is something wrong? How do you feel?'

'Not marvellous, but thanks to you, Miss Warner, there's an outside chance I'll live. Now I can string two words together without barking like a hound, I'm ringing to thank you.'

'Only too happy to help,' she assured him, eyebrows raised at the change in his attitude.

'I heated the soup, as per your instructions,' he went on. 'And even cut some bread, but I was too damn feeble to wrestle with the coffee machine so I made some tea. I didn't know I had any tea—'

'I bought it for you.'

'Then I owe you, Miss Warner.'

'You can pay me tomorrow, Mr Tennent. Is there anything else you need?'

'Just a morning paper as you come in, if you would. How do you get here?'

'I walk.'

'Where do you live?'

'Spitalfields. Would you like me to make lunch for you?'

'Don't bother about that. Just the sound of a human voice will do. Wallowing alone with my bug soon lost its appeal.'

Emily frowned. 'The Donaldsons are away, of course, but surely you have other friends who could call round?'

'The two most likely succumbed to the bug before I did—' He broke off to cough, and Emily waited until he was quiet before asking if there was anything else he needed.

'I can get it on my way in, Mr Tennent.'

'Call me Lucas.'

'Not suitable,' she said firmly.

'Why the hell not?'

'For obvious reasons.'

'If you mean because you work for me, that's rubbish,' he said with scorn. 'According to the great and good we live in a classless society these days.'

'It's nothing to do with class,' she said indignantly.

'You said choice of name was up to me,' he reminded her.

'I meant *my* name—' She stopped, wondering why she was making a fuss. 'Oh, all right, whatever you say.'

'Bravo. Now I can go happy to bed.'

'You should be in bed right now.'

'I was speaking figuratively. Apart from staggering out to the kitchen to make my supper, I haven't left my bed all day.' He coughed again. 'I trust you feel suitably sympathetic?'

'Of course I do. I was a fellow sufferer not so long ago, remember. Goodnight. I hope you sleep well. I'll see you in the morning.'

Emily had barely put the phone down when it rang again.

'At *last*, darling,' said Claire Warner. 'I've been trying to get you for the past ten minutes.'

'Hi, Mother. What's wrong?'

'Miles rang here half an hour ago, demanding your address.'

'*No!*' Emily groaned. 'You didn't tell him?'

'Of course not,' said her mother scornfully. 'I didn't even speak to him. Your father answered the phone and wiped the floor with him; told him to leave you alone.'

'Way to go, Dad,' crowed Emily, then sobered. 'Actually, Miles left a message here just now, too. He's got hold of my new number somehow.'

'Oh, *Emily*. Have you given it to someone he knows?'

'Only Ginny. But she wouldn't tell him.'

'I'm sure she wouldn't. How is she?'

'Fine. We had our usual little jolly together yesterday. Though she spent most of it lecturing me.' Emily explained about Lucas Tennent's flu.

Because Claire Warner failed to see why her daughter had to do the man's cleaning in the first place, let alone look after him now he was ill, she expressed whole-hearted agreement with Ginny. 'For heaven's sake, child. It's not all that long since you were down with flu yourself. Amongst other things.'

'Temper, mainly.'

'You're certainly well shot of Miles Denny. I hope Nat hasn't put your name on his door!'

'Of course he hasn't. Nat lets me know if my presence is required when he's around, and Ginny rings me as she's coming down the street and I go down and let her in.'

'Terribly cloak and dagger—like living in a safe house.'

'Nat's house *is* safe.'

'You know what I mean!'

'You read too many crime novels, Mother. I just needed a place in London to get myself together for a bit. And Nat has provided it. I'm very grateful to him.'

'Darling,' said her mother, after a pause. 'Nat's a charming man, but—'

'Oh, *Mother!* Nat is Andrew's friend, not mine at all, really. And he's married to Thea and father to the twins. What on earth do you take me for?'

'At the moment, a very vulnerable girl,' said Claire Warner bluntly.

'I've learned my lesson, believe me.'

'No more men, you mean?'

'Certainly not. I'm off *Miles*, Mother dear, not men in general.'

But afterwards Emily felt deeply uneasy. If Miles had her phone number maybe he could track down her address, too—even have it already. Though if he was brass-faced enough to turn up in person he'd have to get past Nat, and possibly Mark as well, to get hold of her.

Emily had just got down to work on her book when the phone rang for a third time. She groaned in frustration, but at the sound of Ginny's familiar tones she cut through the message to answer.

'Hold it, I'm here.'

'Emily, thank heavens. You've been engaged forever. You'll never guess who came round here this evening!'

Emily sighed. 'I bet I can—Miles.'

'*Yes*. How did you work that out?'

'He rang my parents earlier, but my father gave him a very un-Christian ticking off, according to Mother.'

'Brilliant! That must have been before he came here, then. I was in the shower when he turned up, so Charlie left him cooling his heels in the hall until I deigned to appear.'

'Well done. What did he want?'

'Your phone number and address, of course.'

'You didn't—'

'Of *course* not. Even though he kept hammering away that it was a matter of life and death that he got in touch with you.'

Emily snorted. 'Not a hope.'

'My words exactly. He didn't like it one bit,' Ginny informed her with satisfaction. 'Took umbrage, big-time.'

'What happened then?'

'Charlie showed him the door.'

Emily giggled. Ginny's large husband was by nature imperturbable, unless someone was foolish enough to upset his wife. 'I don't suppose he physically threw Miles out?' she asked hopefully.

Ginny laughed. 'Next best thing: I doubt Miles will pay us a repeat visit. Let's hope he doesn't try to visit you, either. Has he ever met Nat?'

'No. Hopefully he never will, either.'

The idea of Miles tracking her down kept Emily awake for a while, but in the end she slept well enough, and woke with a feeling of anticipation she eventually identified—with alarm—as pleasure at seeing Lucas Tennent again. None of that, she warned herself, and went off to take a shower.

When Emily went downstairs later Nat was in the hall, about to leave for the day. He looked tired and pale, but not, she saw with relief, as depressed as he usually did after parting with the twins.

'How did it go?' she asked warily. 'I didn't like to barge in on you yesterday to ask.'

'The twins flew at Thea, and before she could say a word demanded that I stay for tea.' He smiled crookedly. 'To my amazement, their wish was granted. And the occasion went off surprisingly well, mainly because the twins dominated the entire occasion over the tea and cakes.' He shrugged. 'Who knows? Next time maybe Thea will ask me to supper.'

'Oh, Nat, I do hope so. By the way,' she added, 'my ex left a message on my phone last night.'

Nat's eyes narrowed. 'How the hell did he get hold of the number?'

'No idea. I just hope he doesn't ferret out the address, too.'

'Don't worry, Em. I'll deal with him if he does. Give me a photograph.'

'No can do. I burned them all.'

'Description, then.'

'About your height, but heavier, dark eyes and hair, toothpaste ad smile, and so full of himself you'll recognise him on sight.'

Nat grinned. 'You're still angry with him, then.'

'Livid!' She looked at her watch. 'Must go.'

'You look rather special this morning,' he said, giving her the once-over.

'Things to do after my morning cleaning session,' she fibbed. 'But I'll see to your place this afternoon.'

'Right, I must be off, too.' Nat gave her an evil grin. 'And don't worry, if Mr Denny comes knocking I'll throw him out, neck and crop.'

Emily set off for her normal working day with anticipation she firmly dismissed as utter nonsense. Lucas Tennent was feeling rough and needed company; she was merely the person willing to brave his germs. And to brighten him up she was wearing a newish yellow sweater with her jeans, and a touch of make-up. No big deal.

By the time the lift doors opened on the top floor of Lucas Tennent's building Emily had herself well in hand. She was the cleaner. Lucas Tennent paid her wages. For the moment he was feeling so rotten he needed a helping hand. So she would be brisk and efficient, hand over the paper, complete her usual cleaning routine, make lunch for him, then go straight home again.

Emily pressed the buzzer, unlocked the door and called her name. And this time Lucas appeared at once, haggard, the bloodshot eyes dark-ringed, but with a smile of greeting so different from the hostility of the day before it did serious damage to her resolutions.

'Good morning, Emily Warner. Good of you to come.'

'I'm always here on Mondays.' She handed him the paper.

'Thank you just the same. But be of good cheer,' he said, leaning in the doorway. 'No need to change sheets and force pills down my throat. I've performed both duties myself, already.'

'Well done.' She took off her jacket and put it on the chest. 'How do you feel?'

'Not wonderful. But better than yesterday.'

Which was obvious from the interest he was taking in her appearance.

'Back to bed now,' she said briskly. 'Read the paper while I tidy up.'

'Forget that. I need conversation. Come and talk to

me for a while—' Lucas broke off to cough, and Emily gestured towards his bedroom.

'Please go back to bed.' She went ahead of him to stack the pillows and turn down the newly changed covers. 'You should have waited for me to do this,' she said severely. 'Because you don't feel so marvellous now, do you?'

'No,' he admitted, and slid into bed with a groan of relief.

'Have you had anything to eat today?'

'I drank some milk.'

'Better than nothing, I suppose,' said Emily, and smiled her approval.

'Cute dimple,' he commented.

'What would you like to eat?' she asked, ignoring him. 'Eggs in some form would be best. Something light to start you off.'

'At the moment I feel too feeble to lift a fork. Later, maybe. When I've got over my exertions.' He eyed her irritably. 'For the moment just sit down and *talk* to me, woman.'

Objecting hotly to this form of address, Emily stood her ground for a moment, then sat down on the chair beside the bed. 'Oh, very well. What shall I talk about?'

'You.'

She grimaced. 'Boring subject.'

'I disagree.' He slid further down in the bed. 'Tell me what you did before the domestic engineering.'

'I worked in a commercial retail agency—I told you it was boring.'

'Emily, that sexy voice of yours could recite the phone book without boring me.' He threw up a hand at her scowl. 'Sorry, sorry. Go on. Tell me why you switched careers.'

She shrugged. 'I lived for a while with a man who worked in the same agency. When we broke up I moved out and packed in my job.'

Lucas lay watching her, his shadowed eyes alert with interest. 'Non-amicable parting, obviously. When was this?'

'Fairly recently. Now, how about that breakfast?'

His mouth twisted. 'I'm a bit wary of eating. It's bloody mortifying to keep dashing away to throw up.'

She nodded sympathetically. 'My mother got a leaflet about flu when I was ill. It said one must try to eat if possible. So will you try?'

'On one condition—that you keep me company while I do.'

'If you insist.'

'Not at all. I'm asking you nicely!'

Emily laughed and went off to the kitchen. When she returned to the bedroom with a laden tray she found Lucas waiting with barely concealed impatience, the daily paper unopened beside him. 'Sorry I was so long,' she said breathlessly. 'I'm used to cleaning your kitchen, but not cooking in it.'

'Which you shouldn't be doing at all,' he said irritably.

'Of course I should.' She laid a clean towel across his chest. 'Better use this now you've made the effort to change your bed.' She handed him a fork and a plate of scrambled eggs on toast, then feeling a little awkward sat down again. 'Salt, pepper?' she asked. 'I seasoned the eggs a bit, but you might want more.'

'They're perfect,' he said, tasting them. 'Now, entertain me while I eat. I can tell you're not a Londoner. Where do you come from?'

'Chastlecombe, in Gloucestershire.'

'Snap—same county,' he informed her with a grin. 'We're both country bumpkins, then.'

Anything less like a country bumpkin than Lucas Tennent was hard to imagine. Even lying in bed, haggard and feverish. 'Speak for yourself,' she said pertly, then bit her lip.

'What now?' he demanded.

'I keep forgetting.'

'Forgetting what?' His eyes narrowed. 'Oh, right. Me boss, you slave.'

Emily glared at him. 'I wouldn't put it quite like that!'

'I should bloody well hope not,' he said forcibly, and eyed his empty plate in surprise. 'That was good. Thank you.'

Emily took his plate to the kitchen, then returned shortly afterwards with two mugs of coffee. She handed one to Lucas, then resumed her place in the chair. 'You look a little better now,' she said with approval.

'I feel it.' He drank with relish, then settled back against his pillows. 'So tell me more, Emily. What course are you doing?'

She winced. 'I lied about that.'

'Did you now?' he said, eyeing her flushed face with amusement. 'So what exactly *are* you doing on that laptop of yours? Hacking into state secrets?'

'Nothing so exciting. I'm trying my hand at a novel. I make a sort of rough draft of the next bit in my head while I'm cleaning, then get it down on my laptop later. But if I hadn't been stupid enough to lie to you when you caught me,' she added bluntly, 'I wouldn't be telling you this. No one else knows, not even my family.'

'My lips are sealed,' he assured her, hand on heart. 'But why the secrecy?'

Her chin jutted. 'I experienced a pretty humiliating form of rejection recently. If—or more likely when—the manuscript's rejected, too, I'd rather no one knew about it.'

CHAPTER THREE

LUCAS eyed her with respect as she got up to refill his coffee cup. 'You're a lady of surprises, Emily.'

She shook her head. 'Not really. All my life, until recently, I did everything by the book.'

'What happened then?'

'Miles Denny happened.' Emily sat down again. 'My family disapproved. They don't like him.'

'I don't either.'

She laughed. 'You haven't met him.'

'I don't have to.' He frowned. 'Emily, I've got a name, but you haven't used it yet. I thought we'd sorted that out.'

She gave him a fulminating look, and jumped to her feet. 'Right—*Lucas!* I'm going to clear up now.'

'Don't go yet! Please?' His eyes met hers with a persuasion she found impossible to resist.

'I'm still going to clear away and so on,' she said firmly, picking up the coffee tray. 'But I'll come back afterwards for a few minutes. Then you should try to sleep.'

'I can do that when I'm alone,' he said testily.

While Emily loaded the dishwasher later she fought a losing battle with her common sense. She'd achieved her aim in coming here to check on Lucas Tennent, feed him, and make sure he wasn't any worse. So she should go home once she'd finished her usual routine. But it was such balm to her dented ego to have a man like Lucas Tennent pleading for her company. Besides, she thought, brightening, it was all an aid to research. The more she saw of him, the more her fictional hero would take shape.

She paid the living-room some attention, made sure the kitchen was immaculate, then cleaned the bathroom in the hall to complete at least part of her usual routine for Mondays. Afterwards she brushed her hair, used a lipstick, then went to rejoin Lucas, who regarded her with bloodshot, accusing eyes.

'I thought you'd gone,' he said, his jutting lip so much like young Tom Sedley in a strop that Emily bit back a smile.

'What's so funny?' he demanded.

'You reminded me of someone.'

He scowled. 'Not the much-disliked Miles?'

'No. I'm very fond of this someone.'

'Who is he?'

'Son of my landlord.'

'One of the twins?'

'You remembered,' she said, surprised, and sat down in the armchair.

'I remember everything you've told me so far,' Lucas assured her. 'I've felt too lousy to read, or watch television, so I lie here and think about you.'

'Time I was going,' she said hastily, and got up, but he lunged swiftly and caught her hand.

'I was *not* coming on to you. I meant that you interest me.'

Her eyebrows rose. 'Is that a compliment?'

'It's the truth,' he said simply, and released her hand.

Appeased, Emily resumed her seat. 'By the way, Lucas, the new number I left for you is unlisted. My family have it, of course, and my closest friend, but—'

'Not Miles,' he said, nodding.

'That's the problem. He's got hold of it somehow. He rang me last night.'

His eyes narrowed. 'Did you speak to him?'

'No. I just listened while he left a message. He tracked the number down somehow. Now I'm afraid he'll find out where I'm living.' She shivered at the thought.

Lucas frowned. 'Emily, are you afraid of this guy?'

'Certainly not. I just don't want to see him again.'

'Why did you leave him?'

Her lips tightened. 'The usual reason.'

'Another woman?'

'One that I know of personally, but probably a lot more that I don't.' She shrugged. 'A boring little tale.'

He settled more comfortably against the pillows. 'Tell me about your family instead.'

Preparing to lie about some fictitious appointment, Emily hesitated. Lucas Tennent was enjoying her company. And she was enjoying his. But she had no illusions. Without his dose of flu none of this would be happening.

His heavy eyes narrowed as he watched her face. 'You're about to say you can't stay. Are you due at the Donaldsons'?'

'No, not today. But I should be going home.'

'Don't tell me we're back to this "upstairs, downstairs" garbage again?' he demanded irritably.

'You should be resting.'

'I can do that after you're gone.' He gave her a cunning look. 'I could pay you overtime.'

'Certainly not,' she snapped, bristling.

He grinned. 'Thought that would do it. Right, then. Stay for a while. Talk to me.'

Disarmed by the grin, Emily gave in, and at his prompting provided Lucas with a brief résumé of her

background—father a retired clergyman, mother a leading light in the local history society and devourer of
crime novels. 'A combination with drawbacks,' she said
wryly. 'Mother wasn't keen on my move to Spitalfields
because it was once a favourite haunt of Jack the Ripper,
though she's interested in the Roman skeletons found
there. I also have a brother,' she went on. 'Andrew is
head of the physical education department in the school
he once graced himself in company with my landlord,
Nat Sedley. They've been close friends ever since, which
is why Nat offered me a room in his house when I left
Miles.'

'And is your landlord married to the mother of his
twins?' Lucas asked casually.

'Yes. But there's a rift. Thea lives with the children
in their house near Chastlecombe and Nat lives alone up
here. But he desperately wants his life with Thea back.
He gets the twins on alternate weekends but it cuts him
to pieces to part with them every time. He's a colleague
of Liz Donaldson, your neighbour, by the way.' She
smiled a little. 'He interrogated her pretty thoroughly
about you before I was permitted to take the job.'

Lucas gave her a cynical look. 'Are you *sure* this man
still loves his wife?'

'Nat was merely acting on Andy's behalf to make sure
you were a suitable employer for the little sister.' She
smiled demurely. 'Happily, you passed muster.'

He laughed, then put a hand to his head, wincing. 'I'm
pleased I made the grade.'

'Is your head bad?' she said with sympathy.

'Only when I laugh.'

'I'll give you some more pills, then you really should
try to sleep.'

'If I do, you'll disappear.' He gave her a cajoling look.

'If I promise to sleep for a while will you stay this afternoon, and have tea with me later? In the meantime, put your feet up, watch television, or read. Take anything you like from my shelves. Another time,' he added slyly, 'you can bring your laptop and work here.'

'There won't be another time. You'll be better soon.'

'No, I won't,' he said promptly. 'I'm very ill.'

'In that case, you'd better call a doctor.'

'I don't want a doctor. I just want you to stay for a while. Though God knows I don't blame you for wanting to run,' he added with sudden self-disgust.

Emily eyed him in silence for a moment, then nodded reluctantly. 'Oh, very well. I'll stay until six, but then I really must get back, otherwise there'll be no point in going. I'm due at the Donaldsons' in the morning. They come back tomorrow.'

'Don't go back. Stay the night in my spare room. I meant it just now,' he added quickly. 'I'll happily pay the overtime.'

She gave him a scornful look, took two pills from his bedside drawer, poured bottled water into a glass and handed it to him. 'Every drop, please.'

He obeyed, then gave her a smile which unglued her knees. 'Thank you, Emily. I promise I won't mention money again.'

In contrast to the stark, minimalist effect preferred by the Donaldsons, Lucas Tennent's taste ran to uncluttered comfort. Because the converted loft gave maximum living space but presented a problem with storage, he'd solved it by investing in a collection of chests, some of them modern, others brassbound and antique. In places the old honey-coloured brick of the walls had been left exposed, in others plastered and painted amber, the few pictures hung on them modern, bright slashes of colour.

And in the short time she'd been working there Emily had come to love every inch of it.

Her only time spent in the vast, split-level living area had been to put it in perfect order as part of her cleaning routine. But now, while the washing-machine was on its dry cycle, Emily settled down on one of the deep, tempting sofas and began to read. Before long the words started to run into each other and at last she gave up, tugged off her shoes and curled up, her head on one of the cushions. She set a mental alarm clock to wake up after half an hour, so she could check on the invalid, but woke with a start to find Lucas Tennent looking down at her.

'I'm terribly sorry,' she said penitently, scrambling to her feet to put her shoes on.

'It was so quiet I thought you'd gone home after all, so I came to investigate.'

'You shouldn't be out of bed,' she scolded, and took his arm to shepherd him back, then dropped it again in alarm when she felt the heat of his skin scorch through the clothes.

'Do that again,' he said, grinning. 'I like it.'

Emily gave him an exasperated glare. 'If you'll go back to bed, I'll make tea.'

'Tea for two,' he said firmly, then turned away to cough.

'You see? Go back to bed—Lucas, *please*,' she begged, and flushed at the look he gave her.

'For you, Emily, anything,' he assured her and, still coughing, went off towards his bedroom.

She went to the kitchen to make tea and toast the crumpets she'd included in her shopping. When she took the tray into the bedroom Lucas was waiting, bolt upright against neatly stacked pillows in his newly tidied bed. His ashen face sported streaks of hectic colour, which worried Emily very much, but she smiled at him as she put the tray down.

'Feeling better?'

'Not a lot,' he admitted, and gave a rueful look at the dish of crumpets. 'I hate to be ungrateful, Emily, but I'm not hungry.'

'OK,' she said without fuss. 'Just the tea, then.'

He downed the tea thirstily, then lay back against the pillows as though the mere exertion of drinking had exhausted him. 'I feel so bloody feeble. Were you like this?'

'Yes. But my mother called the doctor, who gave me antibiotics for my chest infection. So I soon got better,' she added significantly. 'Look, Lucas, your temperature's up and I can hear you wheezing from here. You need a doctor. Do you have one I can ring?'

'It's just flu,' he said testily. 'I don't need a doctor—' He broke off to cough again and Emily handed him a box of tissues, then looked at him in question as the phone rang.

'Answer it, please,' he gasped.

Emily picked up the receiver and said a cautious hello.

'Alice Tennent here,' said an attractive voice. 'Is Lucas there?'

Emily gave the receiver to Lucas, who lay with sweat beading his forehead as he battled to control his cough. He croaked a hoarse greeting, then went off into another paroxysm of coughing and handed the receiver back. 'My sister—explain,' he gasped.

'I'm afraid your brother's feeling very unwell, Miss Tennent,' said Emily.

'Sounds as though he's dying! Has he seen a doctor?'

'He refuses to call one,' she said, defiant as she met

the glare in the invalid's eyes. 'And I'm pretty sure he's got a chest infection.'

'Right. Hand him over, please.'

Emily thrust the phone at Lucas, then watched in some amusement when he disagreed in violent protest with his sister before handing the phone back. 'She wants to speak to you,' he growled.

'Who, exactly, *am* I speaking to?' asked Alice Tennent pleasantly.

'Emily Warner, your brother's cleaner,' she said baldly, ignoring the look of impotent wrath on the invalid's face. 'I stayed on this afternoon because I was worried about your brother.'

'That's extraordinarily kind of you! Look, Mrs Warner—'

'Miss, actually.'

'Right. I've just told Lucas that if he won't behave I'll send Mother up to look after him. In which case she will certainly catch the bug herself. Naturally Lucas won't hear of that. I'd come myself but I'm ringing from Italy. Can you contact a doctor and stay with Lucas until he arrives?'

Emily had no hesitation. 'Of course, Miss Tennent. If the doctor thinks it necessary I can even stay the night.'

'How very kind. Thank you. That's a load off my mind. Now, put Lucas back on and I'll read the riot act.'

But this time Lucas was surprisingly acquiescent as he listened, eyes fixed on Emily. 'Did you mean it about staying the night?' he demanded as he handed the phone back.

'Of course I did.' She picked up the tray. 'Where will I find your doctor's number?'

'In the address book on my desk up in the gallery.' He mopped at the perspiration standing out on his forehead. 'I've only seen him once. Maybe he doesn't do house calls.'

'He'd better,' said Emily darkly.

She stated Lucas's problem to a receptionist, gave directions to the flat, then went back to Lucas, who by this time was looking ghastly.

'A doctor's coming shortly,' she told him.

'Dr Barnett?' he croaked.

'They didn't say. Probably whoever's on call.' Emily eyed him with misgiving. 'How do you feel?'

'Not great. It hurts to breathe,' he said hoarsely. 'I don't get it. I felt so much better earlier.'

Emily went into his bathroom, collected a towel, dampened a washcloth and went back to the invalid. 'I'll just wipe your forehead,' she said briskly.

'You don't have to do this,' he protested.

'No,' she agreed. 'But you'll feel better if I do.' She mopped him up, dried him off with the towel, poured water into a glass and handed it to him. 'Down the hatch.'

'I might be sick again,' he protested wildly.

'You're sweating so much you'll get dehydrated if you don't drink.'

He gave in and took a few sips of water, then gave her a wry, twisted smile. 'I bet you're sorry as hell you stayed behind on Friday.'

'Certainly not. I'm glad to help.' She looked him in the eye. 'How would you have managed otherwise?'

He smiled ruefully. 'A question I've been asking myself all day, Emily Warner.'

'I'm not sure how long the doctor will be,' she said. 'Otherwise I'd say another change of bedclothes was a good idea. But maybe it's best if you stay the way you are.'

'So he can see how poorly I am?' he mocked.

'Exactly.' Her tone was casual, but underneath Emily was worried. Lucas's forehead had been so hot the wash-cloth had steamed as she mopped him with it, reinforcing her fears about pneumonia. So far she'd functioned on common sense and her own experience, but committed to an overnight stay she felt in urgent need of profes-sional advice.

'Lucas,' she said apologetically. 'I'm probably the only person you've met who doesn't own a cellphone. May I make a phone call?'

'Of course. Use this phone, if you like, or one of the others out there if you want privacy,' he said, his breath rasping in his chest.

She smiled her thanks, and stayed where she was to contact Nat.

'Hi, Emily here. I'm just letting you know I couldn't make it this afternoon, and I won't be back home to-night.'

'No need to clock in and out, Em,' Nat assured her.

'I know that,' she said, colouring under the sardonic gaze trained on her face. 'But I thought I'd better ex-plain.'

'Much appreciated,' he said warmly. 'I'll see you when I see you, then.'

'Right. Apologise to Mark for me.' Emily put the phone down, her eyes defiant. 'My landlord,' she said shortly.

'Are you *sure* there's nothing going on between you—?' Lucas broke off, coughing, and flapped his hand at her in apology. 'Sorry. None of my business.'

She glared at him. 'I'll have to skip my other cleaning jobs this afternoon, and since living in Nat's house I've never stayed out overnight before. So it seemed like common courtesy to explain. But you're right—it *is* none of your business.'

He lay panting, his feverish eyes bright with amusement. 'That's better!'

'What do you mean?'

'You forgot the paid underling bit.'

'Oh.' Emily thrust her hair behind her ears. 'Sorry,' she muttered.

'Don't be. I like pushy women.'

'In that case, for heaven's sake listen to this one and just lie there quietly until the doctor comes.'

But it was almost two o'clock before the doorbell rang, by which time Lucas looked so ill Emily was secretly frantic.

'Dr Hall,' announced a brisk young woman when Emily opened the door. 'I came as soon as I could, but we're busy. How's Mr Tennent?'

'Not too good. Thank you so much for coming.' Emily led the way to the bedroom and ushered the attractive young doctor inside. 'Dr Hall, Lucas,' she announced, and hid a smile at his open dismay at the sight of a female GP.

'Sorry to bring you out, Doctor,' he said hoarsely, but the young woman shrugged as she took a stethoscope from her bag.

'Goes with the territory, Mr Tennent. Sit up, please.'

She hoisted up Lucas's T-shirt to give his chest and back a thorough examination, checked his pulse and his blood pressure, looked in his ears and down his throat, took his temperature, then sat down on the chair by the bed to write a prescription. She tore it off the pad, took a strip of bubble-packed pills from her bag and handed both to Emily.

'I'll give you a few antibiotics to start him off. You can get the script filled tomorrow for the rest.'

'Will I live, Doctor?' wheezed Lucas.

'It's just a respiratory infection, so if you follow the instructions, yes.' She turned to Emily. 'See he gets plenty of fluids, sponge him down if he gets too hot, and he'll need to take the pills at four-hourly intervals to start with. Right through the night, if possible. Tomorrow he can go on to four times a day.'

'Thank you,' said Emily. 'I'll see you out.' Once in the hall, out of Lucas's range, she confronted the doctor. 'Is there any danger of pneumonia?'

'I doubt it. Normally, Mr Tennent's obviously very fit, so once the medication kicks in he'll get better quite quickly.' Dr Hall eyed her surroundings curiously. 'What does he do for a living?'

'Works for an investment bank.'

'Ah. Long hours, lots of stress. Rather like my job— only much better paid. Make it clear that he won't be back at the grind until he's finished the antibiotics.'

Emily smiled awkwardly. 'We're not really on that kind of footing. I'm just his cleaner.'

Dr Hall looked taken aback. 'Oh—sorry. Is there someone else who can look after him?'

'Only me for the time being.' Emily eyed the doctor questioningly. 'Or do you think he needs professional nursing?'

'Not at all. If you're willing to look after him he'll be fine. I'd better be off; more calls to make.' She smiled. 'Good luck, then.'

'I'll probably need it! Goodbye, Doctor.'

Emily went back to the bedroom, poured water into a glass and handed Lucas the first of his antibiotics.

'What if I throw it up?' he gasped after he'd taken the pill.

'You won't,' she said firmly. 'Think positively.'

'Yes, Nurse.' He managed a smile. 'Bossy creature. Just like the doctor.'

'She looked very tired,' said Emily reprovingly.

'I'm very grateful to her,' he wheezed. 'To you, too,' he added. 'How can I repay you?'

She smiled awkwardly. 'I just need the money I spent on your shopping.'

Lucas looked appalled. 'Hell, of course you do. Fish in the top drawer of that chest for my wallet. Take what you want.'

Emily went out quickly, her colour high. But there was no point in false pride. She would look after Lucas Tennent for a while, but she couldn't pay for his food as well. She took the till receipt for the shopping from her bag and went into the bedroom. 'This is what I spent,' she announced, handing it to him.

'I don't want to see that, woman,' he rasped, tossing it away. 'Take whatever bloody money you need.'

Emily went to the chest, extracted a twenty-pound note from his wallet, took the exact amount of change from her own, and left it on the chest. 'I'll leave you to sleep for a while,' she said colourlessly, and turned to go.

'Emily,' said Lucas.

She turned. 'Yes?'

He smiled ruefully. 'Sorry I snapped.'

She looked at him levelly, noting the high colour and fever-bright eyes. 'I'll be charitable and blame your state of health. I'm in the kitchen if you want me.'

'Stay here with me, Emily—' He began to cough again, this time so violently she rushed across the room to hoist him upright, then gave him more water when the paroxysm was over. 'Please?' he gasped.

'Right,' she said, breathing almost as hard as Lucas as she stacked the pillows behind him again. 'I need some tea. But I'll bring it in here until you settle, if you like.'

He nodded wordlessly, his eyes expressing his thanks, and Emily relented, giving him a wry little smile. 'Would you like anything?' she asked.

'No. Just make your tea. God knows you deserve it—along with anything I possess that takes your fancy.'

'Just tea, thanks just the same.'

'Emily.'

'Yes?'

His heavy eyes held hers. 'This Miles of yours must be a raving lunatic.'

'Not really.' She smiled, deliberately activating the dimple. 'Just your average, standard-issue male.'

CHAPTER FOUR

BY THE time Emily got back to the bedroom Lucas had fallen into a restless doze. She tiptoed out again, filled with misgiving about the night ahead. Lucas Tennent's muscular frame carried very little spare flesh, and she was no weakling. But he was a foot taller and a lot heavier than she was. If he got out of bed in the night and collapsed, it wouldn't be easy to get him back in again. She shrugged philosophically. No point in worrying. Now she was stuck with her Florence Nightingale role she'd just have to manage, whatever happened. And in the meantime there was ironing to do. Normally the bedlinen went to the laundry, but at the present rate of turnover she needed to deal with it herself, and fast.

After a brief spell at the ironing board, Emily checked that Lucas was still asleep. She stood looking at him, decided he was safe to leave for a bit, and abandoned the ironing to run out for the rest of the antibiotics. While the prescription was filled she shopped for a few more basic supplies, then raced back to the flat to find Lucas leaning against the chest in the hall, his sunken eyes hostile.

'Where the hell have you been?' he barked at her.

She stiffened at his tone. 'Shopping.'

To her surprise he gave her a contemptuous glare, staggered back to his room and slammed the door.

Seething, Emily shed her jacket, took the bag of shopping into the kitchen, then marched into the bedroom to confront the invalid, who lay rigid in a bed like a rat's nest. 'I brought you the *Financial Times*,' she said, putting it down beside him.

'I didn't ask for it,' he snarled, and turned his head away.

Emily's fast-diminishing sympathy vanished completely. He didn't pay her nearly enough money for this.

'If you'll sit in the chair for a moment, I'll sort the bed out.'

'It's fine as it is,' he growled.

'You'll be more comfortable,' she insisted.

Swearing under his breath, Lucas heaved himself up, then groaned and sat with head in hands for a moment.

'Let me help you,' said Emily, putting a hand under his elbow, but he shook her off irritably.

'I can manage.' He lurched to his feet and swayed so precariously Emily put out a hand, but he gave her a ferocious glare, collapsed in the chair, and sat with bare, muscular legs outstretched, the breath ripping through his chest with a sound like tearing cloth.

Emily swiftly restacked the pillows, straightened the sheet, folded it down over the quilt and turned back a corner. 'In you get.'

'Why the hell did you put a sheet on?' he said irascibly. 'I get tied up in the bloody thing.'

'Because you're sweating so much,' she said, with what remnant of patience she could muster. 'I can change sheets and covers but I can't do much about the quilt itself, so the bed will stay fresher this way. Now you're up,' Emily added, 'how about a visit to the bathroom?'

Lucas lurched to his feet, eyeing her malevolently. 'I'm beginning to sympathise with the ex-lover. If you ordered *him* around like an army sergeant, no wonder he cheated on you.' He went into the bathroom and slammed the door behind him.

Fighting the urge to hurl something at it, Emily put her shopping away instead and made coffee. She laid a tray, and was about to take it into the bedroom, then thought better of it. Lucas might say he didn't want any coffee. In which case he might well get it thrown at him, invalid or not.

She knocked very pointedly on the bedroom door and went in to find Lucas sitting up against the pillows, scowling.

'You were out shopping for a hell of a long time,' he accused. 'What was so vital that you couldn't exist without it for even a day?'

'The rest of your antibiotics,' said Emily, and slapped them down on his bedside table. 'You were still asleep after I'd done some of your ironing, Mr Tennent, so it seemed a good time to make for the pharmacy before it closed. And, just for the record, I was out for less than half an hour. But I plead guilty to a bit of shopping while the prescription was made up. Frivolous stuff like bread, milk, and so on.'

Lucas's blank dismay was almost comical. 'Emily—' He got no further before a cough seized him, and it was some time before he could speak again. 'Hell, I'm *sorry*,' he gasped. 'I was afraid you'd taken off—and wouldn't blame you if you had.'

'I said I'd stay, so I will,' she said coldly. 'But only until tomorrow, Mr Tennent. Now, I've made coffee, so would you like some?'

He nodded, eyeing her with a look she couldn't quite identify. 'Emily, my crack about the ex-lover was way out of order. I apologise.'

'Forget it,' she said brusquely. When she returned

with a beaker of coffee, Lucas eyed it moodily as she put it down beside him.

'Aren't you having any?'

'Yes, Mr Tennent. In the kitchen, with a sandwich. Would you like something?'

'Yes, you can stop calling me Mr Tennent!'

'I meant,' she said, unrelenting, 'something to eat.'

'No, thanks. Unless,' he added, with the sudden, irresistible smile, 'you've got a slice of humble pie handy?'

But Emily, still smarting over the crack about the army sergeant, was immune to smiles by this time. 'I'll be back later,' she said curtly, and left him alone.

In the kitchen, she ate a cheese sandwich, drank some coffee, finished the ironing, then, in need of a break, went into the living-room to read her book. The combination of cheese, coffee and temper had given her indigestion, which made it hard to concentrate at first. But after a while she calmed down enough to follow the intricacies of the thriller's plot. It was half an hour before she went back to check on Lucas, who looked so ill by this time Emily forgot her anger as she laid a hand on his forehead.

'You're burning up,' she commented, worried. 'I'd better sponge you down.'

'You will not!' he growled.

'I'm just following the doctor's instructions.'

'I'll sponge myself down. Later.'

'Now,' she said inexorably.

Lucas glared at her. 'I'll do it next time I get out of bed.'

'Why won't you let *me* do it?' she said impatiently.

'For obvious reasons,' he said through his teeth.

'You mean because I'm your cleaner?'

'No!' he howled, then regretted it when it brought on another bout of coughing. 'Hell,' he gasped afterwards, lying back with an arm over his eyes. 'How long do these antibiotics take to work, for God's sake?'

'They'll function a lot faster if you co-operate.'

'Tell me what to do and I'll do it.'

'Stay where you are unless absolutely necessary, for one thing,' she retorted. 'How long were you hanging about in the hall before I got back from the shops?'

'Not long,' he muttered behind his arm.

'Too long, obviously. From now on, *Lucas*, will you just stay in bed? Please?'

He took his hand away to look at her. 'Yes, Emily. For you, anything. And I'm not just being bloody-minded. At least, not this time. My objection to the sponging is a man/woman thing. We standard-issue males have our pride.'

She smiled unwillingly. 'Can't you just think of me as a nurse?'

Lucas gave her a long, explicit look. 'Emily, angel of mercy you may be, but you're also a woman. And I'm very much aware of it. And now,' he added, resigned, 'I'm going to incur your wrath and get out of bed. I need to go the bathroom again.' His mouth twisted. 'This is all so blasted intimate. And in entirely the wrong way.'

'I feel as shaky as a newborn colt,' he said later, when he got back into the neatened bed. 'What were you doing before you came to check on me?'

'Reading.'

'You were a long time.'

'Half an hour.'

'Bring your book in here.'

'If I do that you won't sleep.'

'I won't sleep anyway. I need company. Your company.' A great shiver ran through him. 'God, I ache all over. I had no idea flu was as hellish as this.'

'As many as a thousand a day died of it about the time Victoria came to the throne,' Emily informed him. 'But *you* won't, as long as you're sensible. How about some soup?'

'Could we leave that until later? Just stay here with me for a while.'

She hesitated, then gave in. 'All right. But only if you try to sleep. I'll fetch my book.'

On her way back, Emily caught sight of herself in the hall mirror and eyed her reflection with distaste. Looking after an invalid was wearing. Or maybe it was just this particular invalid. Obviously never ill normally, Lucas Tennent was convinced he was at death's door. With a wry shrug Emily pushed her unruly curls behind her ears and went back to him.

'Emily,' said Lucas glumly. 'Now I've given it thought maybe it's not such a good idea for you to spend time in here with me.'

'Infection?' she queried, sitting down in the chair. 'Too late to worry about that. Besides, these days I take multivitamins religiously, as instructed by my mother. And she's right. They seem to work.' She gave him the smile which brought her dimple into play. 'If I get you some tomorrow will you take them, too?'

'Yes,' said Lucas huskily, his eyes on her mouth. 'Smile at me like that and I'll do anything you want.'

Emily turned her startled face away and tried to read. The book was gripping, and curled up on Lucas's sofa in his living room she'd been enthralled by it. But here in his bedroom it was different. Conscious in every fibre of the man in the bed, she kept her eyes glued to the book and forced herself to sit motionless for what seemed like hours.

Her tactics paid off. Lucas was dozing when it seemed safe at last to look, and Emily settled down to read in earnest. When she looked up again his eyes were fixed on her face.

'What is it?' she said at once.

He smiled drowsily. 'I was just thinking how reassuring it is to wake and find you here. But you look tired. Are you sure you're not catching this blasted bug, Emily?'

'Perfectly sure. So let's not go over that again,' she said briskly. 'Now, how about that soup?' She leaned over him to tidy the covers, but he dodged away.

'Don't,' he ordered.

'I just—'

'Just *don't*. In fact,' he added harshly, 'I've changed my mind. You'd better go home. I can dish out my own pills.'

She eyed him in exasperation. 'What's the problem *now*, for heaven's sake?'

'You are.'

Emily moved back, offended. 'I see.'

'You don't see at all!'

She looked down her nose. 'Whatever it is, Mr Tennent, I'm not going home. At least, not today. I'll remove myself from your presence, but I'll stay in the flat because the doctor thought it best and I promised your sister. But only until tomorrow. After that you're on your own.' She turned on her heel.

'Emily!'

She halted at the door, but refused to look round. 'Yes?'

'I know you think I'm an ungrateful bastard, but you'd be safer if you went home.'

Emily sighed as she turned to look at him. 'As I keep telling you, Lucas, I'm unlikely to get the virus again. Now try to rest. I'll be in to see you later.'

He turned his face into the pillow, muttering something unintelligible.

If it hadn't been for her assurances to Alice Tennent and the doctor, Emily would have taken Lucas at his word and gone back to Spitalfields. She was tired, and his mood swings were increasingly hard to take. She went back to the sofa in the living room, consoling herself that it was for one night only. After that the ungrateful wretch could doctor himself.

When Lucas had been left to his own devices for a while, Emily knocked formally on the bedroom door and put her head round it.

'You're still here, then?' he asked hoarsely.

'Brilliant deduction. How do you feel?'

'I don't ache so much,' he said with faint surprise, and smiled a little. 'Maybe I'll live after all.'

'Could you manage some soup now?'

Lucas thought it over, then nodded. 'What kind?'

Encouraged by his first glimmer of interest in food, Emily smiled at him in approval. 'Wild mushroom. I bought two cartons of the fresh kind when I was out.'

'Are you having some?'

'Yes.'

'No point in asking you to come in here while we eat, I suppose?'

'None at all.'

When Emily returned with a mug of soup and some fingers of dry toast Lucas was sitting up against newly stacked pillows, a smug look on his face.

'I saved you the trouble of tidying the bed,' he informed her.

'How kind,' said Emily distantly. She whisked a towel across his chest. 'What would you like to drink afterwards?'

'Whatever you're having,' he said virtuously.

She went back to the kitchen to heat her own soup, wondering how long the perfect patient act would last. Lucas was obviously feeling better after a rest, but from her own experience she doubted that would last as the evening wore on.

Beginning to feel the lack of a proper meal, Emily buttered some thick slices of bread to go with her soup. Afterwards she made a pot of tea, then took some in to Lucas to find he'd eaten everything.

'Good,' she said in approval. She filled a glass of water and gave him an antibiotic. 'This would be a good time to take some paracetamol, too.'

'Whatever you say,' said Lucas, obeying so meekly that Emily looked at him narrowly as she took the empty glass afterwards.

'I'm doing my damnedest to please you,' he said, looking up at her. 'Or hadn't you noticed?'

'Oh, yes. I'd noticed.'

Back in the kitchen, Emily frowned as she perched on one of the stools to drink her tea. This time last week she'd never met Lucas Tennent, yet here she was, looking after a stranger in circumstances so intimate they were normally the prerogative of a partner of some kind. Suddenly restless, she went up the open staircase leading from the breakfast bar to the gallery above. She gazed at the lights of the City for a while, looked up to count stars through the arched glass roof, then went back to the bedroom to find Lucas recovering from a coughing spasm.

'You may find this hard to imagine, Miss Warner,' he said, panting, 'but normally I get up early every morning, row on my machine for a while, then walk to the City. There, amongst other things, my working day includes in-depth research, followed by complex reports on shares to recommend to investors.' He glared at her in self-disgust. 'But right now my legs feel like spaghetti, and I can't even concentrate on the daily paper.'

'I know how you feel. I've been there. But don't worry. You'll soon be back to normal.' Emily looked at her watch. 'Try to rest. I'll be back later.'

Much later, she decided. When it was time for the next antibiotic and a hot drink. And after that he was on his own until two. She yawned and set the alarm on her watch, just in case she dozed off during the evening, then settled down on the sofa to enjoy her thriller in peace. She finished the book just before the alarm went off, got up, stretched, put her shoes on and went to beard the lion in his den. And found that now, when she wanted him awake, Lucas was fast asleep, his hair plastered in lank black strands on his forehead, the white T-shirt transparent with sweat.

'Lucas,' said Emily softly, touching his outflung hand.

He muttered, pulling his hand away, then opened his eyes. And smiled at her.

'Hello,' she said quietly. 'Sorry to wake you, but it's time for your medication.'

Lucas blinked, then heaved himself up, his nose wrinkling in distaste. 'Hell, I'm drenched again.'

Emily went to his chest and took out a clean T-shirt and boxers. 'You'd better sponge yourself down.'

He heaved himself out to sit on the side of the bed. 'At least the soup stayed with me,' he said brightening.

'Progress,' she agreed. 'Hurry up. I'll strip this lot off while you wash.'

Lucas got to his feet, took the change of clothes from her with a word of thanks, and made for the bathroom.

Emily stripped the bed at speed, dismayed to find that the quilt itself was damp. She put the bedlinen in the washing machine and, after a moment's thought, took the down-filled quilt to spread on the under-heated floor in the guest room to air. She borrowed the quilt from the guest bed, added the bottom sheet to conserve linen supplies, and returned to Lucas's bedroom with her spoils to hear the shower hissing in his bathroom.

Nothing to do with me, she thought, shrugging, and set to work. The bed was ready and waiting and the room tidy by the time Lucas emerged.

'I smelt like a polecat. I couldn't stand it,' he said flatly, rubbing at his hair.

'I can understand that,' she agreed, surprising him.

He raised an eyebrow. 'I thought you'd be yelling blue murder when you heard the water.'

'What's the point? I could hardly march in there and yank you out of the shower.' She gave him a militant look. 'But please tell me you own a hairdryer.'

'There's one in the chest in the guest room. For visitors' use,' he added blandly.

'Good. I'll get it. Put your dressing gown on and sit in the chair.'

His eyes gleamed. 'Are you going to dry my hair?'

'Only to make sure it's done properly. I flatly refuse to let you get pneumonia and put all my hard work to waste.'

Emily went off to search in the guest room chest,

which, like all the other chests in the flat, lay outside her normal tidying up jurisdiction. It came as no surprise to find a few items of female underwear in the drawer with the hairdryer. Probably the current girlfriend. Who had to be a very tidy creature. In the short time Emily had been cleaning for Lucas she'd never seen any traces of feminine occupation.

When she got back with the hairdryer Lucas submitted to her ministrations with such blatant enjoyment that Emily thrust her fingers through the layers of glossy black hair as rapidly as she could, keeping the dryer on full heat until Lucas protested.

'Steady on. I've only just managed to cool down.'

'You're done, anyway. Back into bed, please.' Emily thrust her own hair back from her shiny face.

'I feel a hell of a lot better after a shower. Why don't you have one, Emily?' said Lucas, eyeing her with sympathy. 'If you need a change of clothes, borrow something from the guest room.'

Emily stiffened, not at all happy to wear something one of his girlfriends had left behind.

'Ladies who stay the night with me,' he said, reading her mind, 'don't sleep in the guest room. But my sister keeps some things in there. Borrow what you like. Alice won't mind.'

'Thank you,' said Emily shortly, and poured water into a glass, then handed it to him with the pill. 'Would you like something to eat?'

'Please don't bother, Emily—you look worn out,' he said remorsefully. 'I'll be fine now. Have your bath.'

'How about tea and the inevitable toast afterwards?' she suggested, annoyed to find her throat thickening at the touch of sympathy. 'I fancy some myself,' she added, her voice even huskier than usual.

'In that case, thank you.' Lucas gave her a very serious look. 'Look, Emily, I know I'm an awkward swine half the time—'

'*Half* the time?'

He grimaced. 'Most of the time, then. But I deeply appreciate what you're doing for me.'

She gave him a stiff little smile and went off to the kitchen, feeling much too tired to cope with a Lucas Tennent who succeeded so spectacularly when he set out to please.

CHAPTER FIVE

EYEBROWS raised at the labels on Alice Tennent's underwear, Emily restricted herself to some lacy briefs, but otherwise made do with her own clothes. Later, showered and dressed, with hair curling damply over the towel round her shoulders, she went to see Lucas, who still looked haggard and sunken-eyed, but visibly less feverish.

'You're better,' she said, pleased. 'Fancy an egg on your toast? Or you could have honey, or jam.'

He thought about it, then shook his head in defeat. 'I'll pass on all three, thanks.'

'Egg for breakfast, maybe?'

'Never mind breakfast, Emily. May I have the pleasure of your company for supper tonight?' he said, and smiled.

Emily's knee-jerk reaction to the smile was to give Lucas Tennent anything in the world he wanted. 'Certainly,' she said, determinedly brisk. 'I shan't be long.'

'You're an angel,' said Lucas later, when she returned with a tray. 'This is perfect for me, Emily, but you should be eating something more substantial.'

'This is just what I want, too,' she assured him as she sat down. It was the truth. She was too tired to bother to cook, or eat, anything more demanding.

'Because I've worn you out,' Lucas said darkly.

'Not at all.' Emily licked her buttery fingers one by one, then stopped, her face hot when his eyes followed

64

the procedure with a relish which made her toes curl. 'More toast?' she said, passing the plate to him.

'You have some, too,' he ordered.

'No more for me.' She got up to hand him the mug of tea.

Lucas took it with a word of thanks, his eyes on her face as she sat down. 'Get some sleep in the other room, Emily. I'll make sure I take the pills on time.'

'I wouldn't sleep if I did,' she assured him. 'So I'll set my alarm and we'll both get some sleep until it rings.'

Twenty minutes later Emily was settled comfortably on one of the sofas. She'd wrapped Alice Tennent's terrycloth robe round her in preference to staying in her clothes, added her own jacket as makeshift cover, and fell asleep almost at once. It seemed like only seconds before the alarm startled her into unwilling consciousness, and disorientated, cold, and only half-awake, she stumbled from the room and went to rouse Lucas.

He was deeply asleep, but to Emily's relief the covers were dry and his forehead free from sweat. She touched his outflung hand.

'Lucas.'

The thick black lashes lifted slowly on unfocused eyes. Lucas stared at her incredulously for a moment, then his eyes lit up and his arms shot up to pull her down to him. Almost in the same movement he rolled over and captured her beneath him, his mouth on hers in a kiss which paralysed her brain.

The hungry, expert mouth took complete possession of hers, kissing her into silence, his tongue invading and caressing, the sheer weight of him holding her body down as he stripped himself. His hands smoothed her robe away to find the warmth beneath, his fingers trailing ribbons of fire over her skin, and she gasped at the exquisite sensation as he caressed her hard, expectant nipples and sent heat arrowing downwards to melt any last shred of resistance. Lucas made a relishing sound deep in his throat as she yielded, his caresses finding erogenous zones Emily had never known she possessed. When his fingers slid between her parted thighs to work their magic on the concealed, throbbing bud, she gave a choked little scream and reared up against him, and Lucas, fiercely aroused, entered her with a smooth, practised thrust which pinned her to the bed. He captured her hands, his eyes burning down into hers for an instant while he held her impaled. Then he began to move, his body urging hers to move with him, and for the next few hot, surging minutes of urgent flesh on flesh, her body responded with total abandon to physical possession so absolute that she clutched his shoulders in frenzy when a powerful orgasm swept over her at last, engulfing Lucas in the same shattering climax before he collapsed on her as though he'd been poleaxed.

For a long, breathless interval Emily lay winded beneath his weight, her body vibrating with the throbbing aftershocks of his lovemaking. But at last, desperate for a deep breath, she pulled herself together and thrust bunched fists at Lucas's shoulders. He rolled clear, trying to take her with him, but she shoved at him so violently he let her go, and without looking at him she tugged at the dressing-gown until she was free. She scrambled out of bed and stood up with her back to him, body and hands shaking as she wrapped the material around her and tied the sash viciously tight. Back still turned, Emily managed to pour a glass of water, took a pill from the pack, blindly thrust it towards Lucas, and rushed out to make for the bathroom in the hall.

She locked the door and sat on the edge of the bath, hands thrust in her hair, breath still heaving through her chest as she fought for calm. I bet Florence Nightingale never had that problem to cope with, she thought, and began to laugh. And couldn't stop even when Lucas began hammering on the door.

'Let me in,' he bawled. 'For God's sake, Emily, calm down and unlock this door, or I'll break it down.'

His threat cut off her hysterics like a douche of cold water. She unlocked the door, turned on the tap in the washbasin and bent her head to splash her face. She felt a towel thrust into her hand and straightened to dry her face, and at last forced herself to face him.

Lucas looked pale and haggard, hair wild and eyes heavy, but in some indefinable way no longer as ill as before.

New cure for flu, thought Emily, and gave him a decisive little smile which stopped well short of her dimple. 'Do you know what my gut reaction to—to all that was?'

His mouth twisted. 'Disgust?'

'Regrettably, no. As was embarrassingly obvious.' She looked him in the eye. 'I'm a practical soul, Lucas Tennent. My first thought was money. Because I can't work for you now. And in my current financial situation that's bad news.'

'You mean all you can think of is *money*?' He frowned incredulously. 'I thought you were hysterical because you felt I'd raped you.'

Emily shook her head impatiently. 'We both know that what happened between us was nothing like rape. —I co-operated with too much enthusiasm for that. Anyway, I thought rapists were motivated by anger.'

'Whereas the only one angry is you,' he said bleakly. 'Do you blame me?'

'No.' He thrust an unsteady hand through his hair. 'Not in the slightest. Is there any point in an apology, Emily? If so, I'll grovel.' He swallowed, his eyes locked with hers. 'I must have been dreaming of you. Then I woke up to find you there for real, and you know the rest. I was only half-awake at first. But that's no excuse. Once you were in my arms I couldn't have let you go if the roof had fallen in.'

'Maybe it's the antibiotics—' She glared at him. 'Please tell me that you took that one just now?'

'Of course I didn't,' he snapped. 'I was too concerned about you.'

'Then go and take it now, for heaven's sake.'

'If I do, will you come with me? To talk?'

Her anger drained away. 'All right,' she said listlessly. 'But only after I've had another bath.'

It was some time before Emily, fully dressed and more or less in her right mind, felt up to facing Lucas again.

'Before you ask,' he said swiftly as she went into the bedroom, 'I've taken the pill.'

'Good.' She moved the chair well away from the bed and sat down in it, legs crossed, trying to look relaxed. 'So what do you want to talk about?'

Lucas sat erect in the bed, his eyes holding hers. 'First of all, I apologise again, Emily. It's not a habit of mine to force a woman.'

She eyed him with scorn. 'Oh, come on, Lucas. You didn't force me. I was so sleepy it was more a case of taking me—and my body—by surprise.' She thought about it. 'More a revelation than a surprise, to be exact, especially the last bit. I've never had an orgasm before.'

Lucas looked thunderstruck. 'Never?' he asked at last.

'No. I've always faked it.'

'Surely that didn't go unnoticed?'

She shrugged. 'Miles certainly never mentioned it.'

Lucas shook his head in wonder. 'The more I hear about this guy, the harder it gets to believe you even passed the time of day with him.'

Emily sighed despondently. 'Whatever I felt for him didn't survive the first couple of weeks. But where we both worked everyone knew we'd bought a place together, and I wouldn't admit, even to myself, that I'd made such a disastrous mistake. My parents wanted me to marry someone else.'

'And Miles took you away from him?'

'Sort of. The relationship with Harry was already running out of steam, anyway. He's a solicitor. Lives in Chastlecombe. But when I came to work in London things sort of fizzled out between us. Then Miles came on the scene, in hot pursuit from the first. Very different from cautious, sensible Harry. But, alas, my savings were my main attraction for Miles.' She gave Lucas a wry look. 'I don't have much luck where men are concerned.'

Lucas moved to the side of the bed and leaned towards a suddenly wary Emily. 'Don't look like that. I'm not going to pounce on you again.' He reached for her hand. 'Let's clear the air. Where I'm concerned you needn't worry.'

'About what?'

'Money, for a start.'

She dropped his hand like a hot coal. *'Money?'*

'I meant,' said Lucas impatiently, 'that even if you never want to lay eyes on me again, you can still go on working for me if you want, because normally our paths never cross.'

'Oh, right,' she said dully.

'The other point I'm forced to raise is lack of protection.' His eyes held hers relentlessly. 'Though your only fear on that score where I'm concerned is possible pregnancy.'

She stared back in outrage. 'Isn't that *enough*?'

'Which means that you don't practise contraception yourself.'

'No. I'm one of the awkward ones. The pill disagrees with me.'

Lucas nodded briskly, then winced. 'I must remember not to do that.'

Emily jumped up. 'Please lie back. For a moment I'd forgotten—'

'That I'm ill?' He smiled. 'So had I. How about writing an article for the *Lancet*. New miracle cure for influenza.'

'It's not funny to me,' she snapped.

'Nor to me,' said Lucas quietly, his eyes steady on hers. 'It was miraculous, Emily.'

Secretly, she was in full agreement, but something about the way he was looking at her told her it would be dangerous to admit it. 'Please rest now. When I leave in the morning I want to know you're on the mend. And able to take care of yourself when I'm gone.'

Lucas held out his hand. 'Sit on the edge of the bed for a while, Emily. We haven't finished our talk.'

She shook her head and got up. 'No more talk, Lucas, I'm tired. And it won't be long before I'm back with the next dose of pills.'

'You don't have to,' he said at once. 'I can do that myself.'

'Possibly,' she retorted, 'but I'll be back at six, just the same. Goodnight.'

This time when Emily settled on the living room couch she felt jumpy and out of sorts, and so far from sleep that she gave up after a while and tiptoed into the kitchen for some water. She perched on one of the stools, chin in hands, then turned to see Lucas watching bleakly from the doorway.

'You look the picture of despair, Emily,' he said, coming nearer.

'Not despair, exactly.' She slid off the stool. 'I was just sorting things out in my mind.'

'What things?'

'Dates,' she blurted, then blushed to the roots of her hair.

Lucas reached for her involuntarily, and Emily leaned against him limply. 'When will you know?' he asked.

'End of next week. I'll find out how soon I can take a pregnancy test.'

Lucas tipped her face up to his. 'And give me the result straight away.'

'Of course.' She smiled faintly. 'Lucas, I certainly didn't bargain for all this when I decided to play Good Samaritan.'

'Enough to cure you of all charitable impulses in the future,' he agreed, and smoothed her unruly curls back in a gesture which made her throat thicken. 'Go and get some rest, Emily. I promise to take my pill at six.'

'I couldn't sleep if I did,' she said, backing away.

'Neither could I.' His eyes met hers. 'The memory of making love to you, Emily Warner, will give me insomnia for the foreseeable future.'

'I bet you say that to all the girls,' she said wearily.

'You couldn't be more wrong.' He shivered and Emily hurried to take his arm.

'Will you please go back to bed?' she scolded. 'I absolutely forbid you to have a relapse.'

'If I did would you stay to look after me?'

'Certainly not! Because you're going to be fine from now on. Though you might feel a bit down for a while,' she warned. 'I certainly did.'

'Without you on hand I'll be more than just down.' In the bedroom Lucas gave her a dark look as he slid beneath the covers. 'Are you really going to abandon me in the morning, Emily?'

'I have work to do,' she reminded him. 'But after I've finished at the Donaldsons' I'll look in on you before I go home.'

Emily made sure Lucas took the medication at six, then retreated to the sofa for an hour to worry about taking the morning-after pill neither of them had mentioned. If her intolerance to contraceptive pills was anything to go by, the effect of such a huge dosage of hormones would be unpleasant in the extreme. But better that than a possible pregnancy. Not that one solitary experience of love, sex, or whatever spin one put on the episode with Lucas, need necessarily result in a baby. And even if it did it wasn't the end of the world. She bit her lip. Who was she kidding? She couldn't bring up a baby in her room in Nat's house. The two flights of steep stairs alone vetoed that. She would just have to find somewhere else. Because for several reasons, her father's calling among them, she couldn't face the idea of returning pregnant and single to Chastlecombe.

At last Emily could stand it no longer. She got up, made use of one of the new toothbrushes Lucas kept in the main bathroom, then went into the kitchen to make coffee. Overcoming reluctance to face Lucas by the light of day, she put her head round his door and found him sitting upright against his pillows, reading the *Financial Times* from the day before.

'Good morning,' he said, abandoning the paper. 'You look shattered, Emily.'

'I'm never very bright in the morning,' she confessed. 'How do *you* feel?'

'A damned sight better than I did yesterday.' He sniffed the air. 'My olfactory powers are back to normal, for a start. Do I smell coffee?'

'I'll bring you some right away.'

'Bring yours as well and sit with me,' commanded Lucas. 'We need to talk.'

'Yes, we do,' Emily agreed. When she got back she handed him a steaming beaker, then sat down with her own. 'First, the morning-after pill,' she said baldly. 'I'd better find a doctor today and ask for one.'

'No way!' he said forcibly. 'Alice's flat-mate vomited for days after taking that, and still stayed pregnant. With your intolerance to contraceptive pills, Emily, God knows what a high-voltage dose of hormones would do. Leave the outcome to me. Please.'

'We don't know there's going to be an outcome yet,' she said irritably.

'True. But no morning-after pill. Emily, promise me.' His eyes met hers with such intensity that she nodded, secretly relieved to have the decision taken from her.

'All right, let's talk breakfast instead. How about some eggs?'

'Yes. If you have some, too. In here. With me.' Lucas lay back against his pillows, smiling with persuasion she couldn't resist.

Emily nodded again, afraid, as so often lately, to trust her voice. She picked up the tray and made for the door, clearing her throat. 'How do you want the eggs?'

'The way you like best,' he said promptly. 'What time are you due at the Donaldsons'?'

'They won't be back until late this evening, so I'll go over there after you've taken the next dose.'

'I'm perfectly capable of looking at a clock and swallowing the damned thing myself,' he informed her.

'Good,' she said, unmoved. 'From then on you'll have to.'

Emily returned later with a tray. She gave Lucas a glass of orange juice, then handed over his omelette and sat down to eat her own.

'Wonderful,' said Lucas indistinctly and peered at her plate. 'Yours is much smaller than mine.'

'I'm not the invalid in need of nourishment—careful, don't eat so quickly.'

'Yes, Nurse,' he said, and gave her a smile which made her heart contract.

'Perhaps you'll fancy something more filling later on,' she said huskily. 'I'll do some shopping while I'm out. What would you like?'

'If I'm to cope with it myself, something basic like soup,' he said, with a melancholy sigh.

'Can't you cook, then?'

'I can, if absolutely necessary. But at the moment I'm a bit deficient in the energy department—for cooking, anyway,' he added, looking her in the eye.

Emily jumped up to take his empty plate, her face hot. 'Right. Soup it is.' She looked around her in disparagement. 'Tomorrow you can retreat to the sofa for an hour while I sort this room out.'

'Tomorrow?' demanded Lucas, brightening. 'I thought you were abandoning me for good, today.'

Emily shrugged, resigned. 'I suppose I'd better come back tomorrow. But not for long,' she added, when his eyes, no longer bloodshot, gleamed like jet in satisfaction.

'I'll take whatever crumbs of your company you'll give me,' he said, with unconvincing humility.

She grinned and went off to the kitchen, sobering quickly as she made tea. This intimacy of sharing meals in the bedroom had to stop. It smacked too much of a relationship which didn't actually exist. And if there were any 'outcome' to the episode in the night, some share of the blame was hers. Lucas hadn't asked her to come round to look after him. She couldn't deny that the enforced intimacy of the past few days had done away with the employer/servant barrier she'd tried to put up between herself and Lucas Tennent. But the fact remained—whatever the outcome, they were still virtual strangers.

She went into the bedroom, gave Lucas his tea, then sat down.

'How do you feel?' she asked. 'Truthfully.'

'A lot better. Yesterday I thought I was dying. Today I'm very much alive.' He smiled at her. 'A combination of medical science and your tender loving care, Emily. No man could ask for more.'

'Good. I won't feel so guilty when I leave you on your own, then.'

His smile vanished. 'I'm going to miss you like hell.'

'Nonsense,' she said, getting up. 'Until last Friday you'd never set eyes on me.'

His eyes gleamed. 'Why can't I get my head round that?'

'Because you're under the weather. Once you're fighting fit and juggling with stocks and shares again, or whatever it is you do—'

'I'll still feel grateful to you, Emily. Nor will I forget,' he added.

She sighed impatiently. 'We're back to the "outcome", I suppose.'

Lucas stabbed her with a look like black ice. 'You don't have some hare-brained idea about keeping me in the dark, by any chance?'

'No.' Though she'd certainly considered it. 'I promised I'd let you know, so I will.' Her eyes flashed. 'But until then, could we drop the subject, please?'

'For the time being only.' Lucas eyed her moodily. 'Must you clean at the Donaldsons' today? You need a rest.'

'It won't take long to leave them a few supplies and make sure everything's shipshape for their return. I did their place thoroughly last Friday.'

His eyes gleamed. 'Eventful day, last Friday!'

Emily gave him a wry smile of agreement and got up to take their mugs. 'Stay in bed, please, Lucas. Take advice from an old hand. You might feel better right now, but leave it for a day or two before you're up all day.'

He scowled. 'I'll go raving mad!'

'Nonsense. There's a radio and a television in here, and a stack of books by your bed,' she said impatiently. 'Be sensible, Lucas. I'll bring you a daily paper when I come back to check on you.'

'How long will you be?' he demanded, looking so gloomy that Emily laughed at him.

'As long as it takes!'

She gave Lucas his pill, provided him with bottled water and orange juice, then went off to do some shopping before her stint at the Donaldsons' flat. After putting the supplies away there, she made sure everything was in order, watered the plants, left a brief note on the kitchen memo-pad to say Lucas had flu, then went back to him.

Emily let herself back into the flat as quietly as she could, put her shopping away, peeped into the bedroom, frowned to find it unoccupied, then gave a smothered screech when Lucas caught her in his arms, spun her round, and kissed her soundly.

'Don't *do* that!' she exploded, shoving him away with furious hands. 'Why are you out of bed?'

'The obvious reason.' He blinked suddenly and steadied himself against the chest at the end of the bed.

'You see?' she said fiercely. 'Crime doesn't pay, Lucas Tennent. I bet your head's spinning.'

'Yes,' he admitted meekly, allowing her to help him back to bed. The black eyes gleamed. 'But only from *your* effect on me.'

'You mean you're not as fit as you thought!' She stared down at him in an agony of indecision, then looked at her watch. 'I really must get back to Spitalfields now, Lucas, but if you can mange on your own this afternoon I'll come back later if you like.'

'And if I promise to keep to my own bed will you stay the night?' he said, with a look of such blazing relief that Emily, who had intended nothing of the sort, nodded, defeated.

'Oh, all right. But just for tonight.'

'But don't walk back, Emily. Take a taxi. I'll pay.'

She smiled wryly. 'You'll have to. My budget doesn't run to taxis.'

Before she went, Emily made some coffee and a sandwich and took it in to Lucas with strict instructions to remember his pill at two. 'I'll be back in time for the next dose.'

'I'll manage without you, somehow,' he assured her.

'Go home and have a rest, Emily. The shadows under those big eyes of yours are giving me a guilt complex.'

'You've got some, too,' she retorted, then grinned. 'But if my eyes look big I'm definitely not sickening for anything. According to my brother, I look like a hamster when I'm ill.'

Lucas let out a snort of laughter. 'Typical brotherly comment.'

'Time I went.' She wagged an autocratic finger. 'Once you've taken the antibiotics, have a good sleep.'

'I will, Nurse, if only to pass the time until you're back. And take some money for the taxi.'

'We'll settle up when I get back—'

'Take it now,' he ordered in a tone which sent Emily to the chest to take out his wallet. Lips compressed, she extracted a banknote and showed it to him.

'Right. I'm off.'

'No kiss goodbye?' he said, aggrieved.

'Certainly not! See you later.'

CHAPTER SIX

ON THE way back Emily bought a pregnancy test, and learned she had nineteen days to wait before using it. By which time it would be unnecessary. When she got to Spitalfields she trudged wearily up the two steep flights of stairs to her room, and found a red light on her answerphone. Certain it was Miles, but afraid to erase the message in case it was Lucas, she pressed the button and listened in angry frustration.

'Emily, this is Miles again. As if you didn't know. I need to talk to you. Pick *up*, Emily.' There was a pause. 'All right. Play it your way. But don't think you can hide forever.'

Why not? she thought furiously. She had nothing to say to Miles. Their parting had been so acrimonious she shuddered at the memory. The row between them had escalated to the edge of violence before Miles had gone rushing out of the flat that night. Afraid he might come back any minute, Emily had left a message on her boss's voicemail to say she was ill, and quit London immediately to drive herself and her possessions to Chastlecombe. By the time she'd arrived home in the small hours her fictional illness had become factual influenza, and as soon as she'd recovered enough to make conscious decisions she'd sent in her resignation. Apart from frantic phone calls to her parents' home, when he was told Emily wanted nothing to do with him, she'd heard nothing since from Miles until his messages on her new, unlisted telephone.

Emily erased the latest, rang to order a taxi for five-thirty, then changed her sweater for a T-shirt and went downstairs to make an overdue start on Nat's rooms. She worked steadily for a couple of hours, then went up to the first floor to perform the same service for Mark. Tired and hot afterwards, and filled with an overwhelming desire to crawl into bed, she swallowed a cup of black coffee instead. Once the caffeine had done its work, she packed an overnight bag, stood under a warm shower for a while, then went back to her room to treat her hair to some styling for once. She gathered it up into a loose, curling knot on top of her head, then paid detailed attention to her face. Yawning, she dressed in bronze velvet jeans and black sweater, pulled on black suede ankle-boots, added a vintage black velvet jacket snapped up in a church jumble sale, slung a long black mohair scarf round her neck, then took her belongings downstairs to wait in the hall for the taxi.

Light-headed with fatigue, Emily dozed on the short journey and woke with a start, blinking like an owl when the taxi stopped outside Lucas's building. She paid the driver, hoisted her bag, then went up in the lift and let herself into the flat. She went quietly into Lucas's bedroom to find him sitting in a chair in his dressing-gown, watching a newscast. At the sight of her he came to his feet with a smile of such unguarded delight that Emily felt a giant fist squeeze her heart.

'I'm back,' she informed him after a pause.

'So you are,' he said huskily. 'I've missed you.'

'Did you sleep?' she said breathlessly.

'Yes. Did you?'

'No. I had a shower instead.'

'Will you hit me if I said I did, too?'

She smiled ruefully. 'Not much point, now. How do you feel?'

'All the better for seeing you, Emily Warner.' He moved closer. 'You still look tired.'

'I had a few things to do,' she said, backing away.

'Working on your laptop?'

'No. Just a bit of tidying up.' Emily looked at her watch then took off her coat. 'I'll put this away, then I'll bring you a drink so you can take your pill.'

'I was just about to do that,' he assured her virtuously. 'Though I'm delighted you arrived early to remind me.'

'Back into bed, then.'

Emily hung her jacket up on a hook on the guest room door, decided the quilt needed to stay on the heated floor a bit longer, then went into the kitchen to put the kettle on to make a hot drink with lemon juice, honey and brown sugar.

'I thought you'd like this for a change,' she said when she took it in to Lucas.

He sipped experimentally and smiled in appreciation. 'Pure nostalgia. My grandmother used to make this when Ally and I were sniffly kids.'

Emily handed him the antibiotics. 'Chase this down with it and you'll soon be back to normal.' A thought which depressed. Normal for Lucas Tennent was light years away from normal for Emily Warner.

He gulped the pill down, took a swig of the drink, then waved her to the chair. 'Sit down and talk to me. I missed you.'

'You said you slept.'

'I did.' His sloe-black eyes locked with hers. 'But I would have slept better with you for company.'

Controlling a shiver of reaction, Emily sat back in the chair, making a conscious effort to relax. 'Do you think that's why I agreed to come back tonight? To sleep with you, Lucas?' she asked bluntly.

He shook his head, smiling. 'I know exactly why you came back.'

She stiffened. 'Oh?'

'Because you just couldn't bear the thought of leaving me all alone and ill.'

Emily grimaced. 'A bit saccharine. Pollyanna was no favourite of mine.'

'If I also said you're sexy as hell would you like that better?' he demanded, then laughed at the outrage on her face. 'I hope you never play poker, Emily.'

She got up, scowling at him. 'I'm going to do something about a meal.'

'I'll only eat it if you come in here and share it with me,' he said promptly. 'Whatever it is.'

Emily shook her head. 'I'll share it with you, certainly, but not in here. If you feel up to it, I suggest you get up for a while and have supper on a tray.'

Lucas eyed her narrowly. 'Does that mean you're never going to set foot in my bedroom again?'

'No, indeed. In the morning I'm going to give it a good sorting out,' she said briskly.

'Emily?'

'Yes?'

He gave her the bone-melting smile. 'Am I allowed to say you're a delight to the eye tonight?'

'Certainly,' she assured him, ignoring her pole-vaulting heart. 'By the way, I forgot to ask. Do you like salmon? The cold, poached variety?'

'As it happens, I do. But for you, Emily Warner, I'd eat anything!'

Emily left him to begin preparations for their simple meal, knowing full well that she looked good tonight.

She'd taken a great deal of trouble with her hair and face, and the clothes she was wearing were simple enough, but they were the kind she wore to go out with Ginny, or to join Nat and the others for a drink. Certainly not the clothes she wore to clean Lucas's flat. Nor the kind she could afford any more. Refusing to analyse her reasons for gilding the lily, Emily prepared tiny potatoes and green beans and put them to cook, then whisked a spoonful of horseradish into clotted cream to accompany the fillets of ready-poached salmon. She buttered slices from a ciabatta loaf, dusted a touch of cayenne over the cream garnish, then tested the vegetables for readiness.

She went into the hall and knocked on Lucas's door. 'Dinner ready in five minutes,' she called.

He came out at once, newly shaved, wearing a heavy sweater and khakis. 'I dressed for dinner,' he said, stifling a cough. 'Can't lie around in a dressing gown when my companion looks so delectable.'

His delectable companion flushed hectically. 'I hope you haven't tired yourself out in the process,' she scolded. 'Go and lie down on one of the sofas. I shan't be long.'

'Emily.' Lucas laid a hand on her arm. 'Relax. Please. I swear I won't jump on you again.'

'I thought we'd decided to drop the subject,' she muttered, face averted.

'We can't pretend last night never happened,' he said quietly, then turned her face up to his. 'But just for *this* evening let's forget I've been ill and you're only here because you promised my sister to stay. I enjoy your company, Emily, so for a couple of hours couldn't you at least pretend to enjoy mine?'

She gave him a very straight look. 'You know perfectly well that I don't have to pretend.'

'Is that why you came back?'

Emily gave him a wry little smile. 'I suppose it must be one of the reasons.'

Lucas had said no more than the truth. She *had* come back because she couldn't bear to think of him alone and ill—also because she'd promised his sister to look after him. But those were the high-minded reasons. The other motive was more basic. She'd just wanted to spend the evening with Lucas. Emily knew that this little interlude was a time apart from their normal lives. Once Lucas was better he wouldn't need her any more.

And pretence didn't come into it when it came to enjoying Lucas's company over the simple meal. It was fun to eat from plates on their knees, sitting together on the same sofa, and, because Lucas had been reading book reviews earlier, arguing amicably over the merits of various writers.

'This morning,' said Lucas, when he laid down his knife and fork at last, 'I wouldn't have believed I could eat a mouthful of that, let alone wolf it down.'

'Flattering to the cook,' commented Emily, finishing her own at a slower pace. 'Though cooking didn't really come into it. Anyone can do something like this.'

Lucas gave her a wry look as she got up to take his plate. 'Not in my kitchen, they don't. No one's ever made dinner for me here before.'

'Really?' Emily eyed him in surprise.

'Really. The ladies of my acquaintance prefer dining out. My sister included.'

Well aware that for a man like Lucas Tennent there would be no shortage of women in his life, Emily controlled an irrational pang of jealousy and went out to load the dishwasher. When she got back with a tray of coffee Lucas sprang up to take it from her.

'Steady,' she warned, as he swayed enough to make the cups rattle. 'Don't get up so suddenly. You're not fighting fit just yet.'

Lucas grimaced as he set the tray down on the low chest in front of the sofa. 'God knows how I'd be at this stage if you hadn't come to look after me.' He sat down and patted the place beside him. 'I suppose I couldn't have a brandy with my coffee?'

'Bad combination with antibiotics,' Emily said firmly, and handed him his cup. 'And no more of this tonight, either, or you won't sleep.'

Lucas leaned back, his eyes on hers. 'I probably won't anyway, with you in the next room.'

'Then I'd better go home.'

'If you do you won't sleep, either.'

'Oh? Why not?'

'Because you'll worry about me.'

His smile was so smugly triumphant that Emily couldn't control a giggle.

'Sophist!' she accused.

'Nevertheless, I'm right. You'd lose sleep over anyone you knew if you thought they were alone and ill.'

He couldn't be more wrong. Up to now, Emily had never experienced such overwhelming urgency to care for someone in the way she did with Lucas. Certainly not with Miles. A discovery which would have saved a whole lot of trouble if she'd made it at the start of their acquaintance.

'You'd better not stay up too long,' she advised him. 'Not for the first time.'

'But if I go back to my bedroom, that's it,' he complained. 'No more Emily.'

She leaned back in her corner, smiling at him. 'You can stay up until you take your last dose for today.'

'Gee, thanks! For that and for a great many other things,' he added, and eyed her musingly. 'Strange to think you've been sharing my flat with me all this time—more or less—without my knowing it.'

'Cleaning, not sharing, Lucas.'

'But you were the one making the place a pleasure to come home to, Emily. A pity I'm rarely home early, or we would have met before.'

She chuckled. 'When we finally did I wanted to sink through the floor. Did you think I was a computer-literate burglar listing your possessions?'

He shook his head, smiling. 'I thought I was halluci-nating.'

'Actually, you were very forbearing, Lucas.'

'A good thing I was,' he said with feeling. 'Otherwise I would have languished alone and ill on my sickbed all this time without a soul to take care of me.'

'I doubt it. Your sister would have arranged for a nursing service.'

Lucas shuddered. 'A thought which makes me all the more grateful to you, Emily.'

She yawned suddenly. 'Sorry! I've had rather a busy day—' She stopped, flushing.

'I thought,' said Lucas suavely, 'that you went home to relax for a while.'

She looked down at her hands. 'I did eventually, but first I had work to do. I was already a day overdue with my other jobs—'

'So you spent the afternoon cleaning for your land-lord!'

'And for Mark, too.' Emily's chin lifted. 'There's ab-solutely no point in glaring at me, Lucas. It's how I earn my living. At the moment, anyway.'

He scowled. 'In the circumstances, surely these guys would have let you off today?'

'Of course they would.' Not that she had the least intention of discussing these particular circumstances with either Nat or Mark. 'But that would have been taking advantage.'

'Do they know you're looking after me?'

'No. Sometimes I don't actually see either of them for days on end. And even when I do I don't have to explain myself to them.' Emily looked pointedly at her watch.

'Don't tell me,' said Lucas, resigned. 'You're about to blow the whistle.'

'It's not up to me, Lucas. If you want to stay up for a while after taking the pills I can't stop you.' She got up. 'I'll fetch you the pill and some water, and I'm leaving a flask of hot lemon drink by your bed in case you fancy it in the night.'

'Thank you—' His eyes narrowed. 'What flask?'

'Mine. I brought it back with me earlier.'

He shook his head in mock wonder. 'You're a paragon, Emily. Did ever think of nursing as a career?'

'Not my kind of thing.' She smiled at him and went off to the kitchen, glad he had no idea that Lucas Tennent was the only man she'd ever met who brought out her caring instincts.

When she got back she was touched to find Lucas had made a nest of cushions in her corner of the sofa.

'Put your feet up and lie there for a while,' he ordered.

'Thanks, it looks so tempting I will.' Emily slid her boots off and curled up with a sigh of pleasure, fixing him with persuasive eyes. 'Lucas, you know all there is to know about me. Would I be overstepping the mark to ask about your background?'

He raised an eyebrow. 'You mean the mark between master and slave?'

'That's the one,' she agreed, smiling. 'If I cross my heart and promise complete discretion, will you give me a brief rundown on the life and times of Lucas Tennent?'

He shrugged. 'I'm not worried about your discretion. I can hardly be of much interest to your friends.'

He hadn't met Ginny, thought Emily drowsily, as he began to talk about his grammar school education, followed by a degree from Cambridge and an MBA. From the start, he told her, he'd been tunnel-visioned about acquiring the best possible technical skills to add to the flair and determination necessary to get on in his profession. He described how he'd begun in a lowly way in research at the investment bank that had offered him his first job, and after rising steadily through the ranks there, had been eventually headhunted by another much-respected banking institution.

'Its continued success in the global market is due to skilful alignment between ambition and resources. In short,' Lucas explained, turning to her, 'an outfit unlikely to crash—'

He smiled ruefully. Emily was asleep. Which allowed his eyes to roam at leisure over the sleeping face framed in escaping tendrils of glossy black hair, the rise and fall of her breasts under the clinging black jersey. Knowing he was to blame for the exhaustion which had finally overtaken her, guilt mingled with the pleasure he took in just looking at her. Filled with a protective feeling new in his experience with women, he got up slowly, careful not to disturb her, then stood frowning in indecision. It was a cold night. Electronically controlled heating or not, Emily would wake shivering at some stage if he left her where she was. Even go down with flu again. He rubbed his chin thoughtfully for a moment, then with infinite care he picked her up and stood still, cradling her in his arms for a moment until he felt steady enough on his feet to carry his sleeping burden.

Relieved to find he was more than capable of transporting one small female a relatively short distance, Lucas made for the guest room, then stood in the open doorway, cursing silently. There were no pillows, the bed was stripped and the quilt was on the floor. For all he knew, maybe he'd gone through his entire stock of bedlinen. And to his disgust he was fast running out of energy to go and check.

Only one thing for it, then. Lucas carried Emily into his own room and very carefully laid her on the bed she had tidied up at some stage during the evening. She muttered indistinctly and he hung over her, braced on his arms, willing himself not to cough. Eventually he straightened with care. Bad idea to collapse on top of her. From her point of view, anyway. But there was still the problem of whether to risk waking her by undressing her, or to leave her as she was. The sweater could stay. But the jeans fitted so perfectly they would be uncomfortable once she was tucked up in bed. Gingerly, he undid her waistband and slid down the zip, waited a moment, then tugged gently and to his relief found the velvet material had some kind of stretch incorporated into it, making it easy to pull off. She made a muffled, protesting sound as he achieved success, then settled into the pillow like a little animal getting comfortable in its nest.

Lucas stood still and watchful for some time. When Emily showed no signs of waking, he went into the bathroom to undress and buried his face in a towel to smother the cough that finally defeated him. When he came out Emily still lay motionless, out to the world, and, taking care not to disturb her, he stretched himself out on the far side of the bed. Resisting the overpowering urge to kiss her flushed, sleeping face, he reached out a hand to switch off the light, then pulled the covers over them and settled down to sleep.

CHAPTER SEVEN

EMILY woke to feel an arm round her waist, and breath hot on her neck, and let out a squeak of fright which woke Lucas up with a start. He snatched his arm away and shot upright, coughing.

'Emily, I can explain,' he panted, meeting her startled eyes. 'Don't be frightened.'

She pushed herself upright, thrusting her hair back from her face. 'I'm not now I know it's you. But for a nightmarish moment I thought it was Miles.'

Lucas let out a heartfelt sigh of relief. 'I was afraid you'd scream and run for your life once you woke up and found yourself in bed with me. But there's a logical explanation, I swear.'

But Emily was less concerned with logical explanations than the discovery that it felt perfectly natural to share a bed with Lucas.

'Don't you want to know why I brought you here?' he demanded. 'And before you ask, nothing happened other than sleep.'

'I know that,' said Emily, surprising him with her dimple. 'Unless you managed to put my clothes back on after you'd had your wicked way. Not counting the jeans, I appear to be fully dressed.'

'You fell asleep on the sofa last night,' he explained. 'I was afraid to leave you there in case you got cold, but when I carried you to the other room there were no sheets on the bed. By that time I was dead on my feet, so I brought you here, even at the risk of mayhem when you woke up. I removed the jeans with great reverence,' he added soulfully.

Emily chuckled, but, suddenly aware that whatever reasons had made it necessary to share Lucas's bed last night they no longer applied now it was seven in the morning, she slid to her feet and made for the jeans folded neatly on the chest. She turned her back on Lucas and pulled the stretchy velvet up over sheer black tights.

'I've never slept in my clothes before,' she muttered, embarrassed now. 'If you don't mind I'll have a quick shower before I make you some breakfast.'

'I don't mind in the least,' he assured her.

Later, when Emily was dressed in the more everyday denims and sweatshirt she'd brought with her, she knocked on Lucas's door before going in.

'A bit late for formality, Emily,' he said, laughing at her. 'Not much point when we've shared nearly every intimacy there is in the past few days. The more romantic of them not of your choice, it's true, and the rest of it certainly not mine. But in the short time since we met we've come to know each other remarkably well.'

Too well in one instance, thought Emily. 'How do you feel today?'

'Better,' he assured her. 'Apart from the odd cough now and then, I'm definitely on the mend.'

'Good.' She smiled in approval. 'I'll bring your breakfast. Then later, when you feel up to it, you can transfer to a sofa while I sort this place out.'

'And after that?'

'I'm going back to Spitalfields.'

Lucas slumped back against the pillows, his eyes accusing. 'Aren't you worried I'll relapse?'

'I can't stay here all the time, Lucas!'

'Why not?' he demanded. 'Are you supposed to be cleaning somewhere today?'

'No,' Emily admitted. 'Not today.'

'Then what's so urgent in Spitalfields that you have to rush back there?'

'My laptop, for a start. I'm not playing at writing a novel, Lucas. I should be working on it right now.'

'Fetch it and work here.'

She gave him a quizzical look. 'Are you really telling me that you can't manage on your own if I go home?'

'No, I'm not,' he admitted with reluctance. 'I'm not feeling totally fit yet, but I'm perfectly capable of heating soup and swallowing pills at the prescribed intervals.' The sloe-black eyes held hers like magnets. 'I'm asking you to stay, Emily, for the simple reason that I'll miss you like hell if you go.'

She turned away blindly and made for the door. 'I need coffee. I'll be back as soon as I can with your breakfast.'

This was getting out of hand. While she made coffee and put eggs to boil Emily made a firm resolution. From now on she wouldn't let those hypnotic black eyes persuade her against her better judgement. The situation was stereotyped enough. The patient dependent on the nurse. But she was not a nurse, and if she had any shred of common sense she would take off today after tidying Lucas's bedroom and come back only when she was due here next. In her official capacity as cleaner. Or, if she were really sensible, not come back here at all.

'Why the heavy frown?'

Emily whirled round, startled, to see Lucas, fully dressed. 'You're up,' she said idiotically, and he grinned.

'So I am. I had to clear out of my bedroom shortly, anyway, so I've come to eat here with you, in the kitchen.' He looked at her steadily. 'But if you object to the arrangement I'll take myself and my breakfast to the living room sofa and leave you in peace.'

Emily put her resolution on hold. 'Of course I don't object. Settle yourself on one of those stools and drink some orange juice while I make toast. I hope you like boiled eggs?'

It was fun to sit perched at the breakfast bar with Lucas, to share coffee and toast and even the eggs, since he insisted Emily ate one of them.

'What do you normally eat for breakfast?' she asked, dunking a finger of toast in her egg yolk.

'Just some fruit juice,' he admitted, following suit. 'Caroline, my assistant, provides me with coffee and croissants when I get in. What about you?'

'At home, under my mother's eagle eye, something like this.'

'And with Miles?'

Emily shrugged. 'I always left long before him to provide *my* boss with coffee and buns.'

'Was the boss man cut up when you left?'

'He said so. He replied to my resignation with a very kind, regretful letter and promised a glowing reference. He even asked me to call in and see him some time. But, for obvious reasons, I'm not going to do that. As far as I know Miles still works there.'

Lucas turned in his seat to give her a searching look. 'I've been thinking about Miles. Exactly why is he ringing you, Emily? Does he want to kiss and make up?'

She scowled. 'If he does he's out of luck. In fact, I'm amazed he wants anything to do with me.'

'Why?'

'Money.' Emily's smile was mirthless. 'My money. When we split up we had a huge row over it. Like a fool I'd given Miles my savings as part of the deposit on the flat. But that night when I asked for it back he said no chance, because he didn't want me to leave, and in any case I hadn't signed anything to prove I'd ever given him any money.' She glowered. 'Like an utter fool I'd trusted him. So I learned the hard way that co-habitation doesn't give a woman the same rights as marriage. Although I paid for our food and household bills while we were together, I didn't contribute to the actual mortgage repayments. And darling Miles had taken out the mortgage in his name only, which means I have no legal rights over the flat we shared and no hope of getting my money back.'

Lucas swore volubly. 'The bastard cheated on you *and* swindled you out of your money? Did you contact a lawyer?'

'Of course. My father got in touch with my solicitor chum right away. But in the end Harry advised us not to pursue it. In his opinion the costs of the case would have come to more than the nest egg I'd handed over to Miles in the first place. Anyway, by that stage I wanted to forget everything about him—*and* his wretched mortgage. And how criminally stupid I'd been.' Emily stared malevolently into her cup. 'I'd saved some of my nest egg myself, but the rest came in presents over the years from my parents, who never have all that much to spare. I could kill Miles with my bare hands every time I think of it.'

Lucas's grasp tightened. 'Look, Emily, if the swine turns up and gives you any trouble at all, tell me right away. I'll sort him out for you.'

'I don't think he will, but even if he does find me in Spitalfields he'll have Nat to contend with first. And don't look like that,' she added impatiently. 'Nat would naturally be first on the scene. It's his house.'

Lucas slid off his stool and lifted Emily down and held her by the elbows, his eyes probing hers. 'If Miles gives you any hassle I'll get a lawyer friend of mine to take out an injunction against him.'

She brightened. 'That's a great idea.'

His grasp tightened a little. 'Tell me the truth. During this row of yours, did Miles get physically violent?'

'No.' Emily gave him a triumphant smile. 'I was the violent one, not Miles. At first that horrible night he just blustered, saying I was making a fuss about nothing. That boys will be boys. Tamara was just a fling. I was important to him.' She shrugged. 'I think his ego just couldn't take it when I said it was over. Then I demanded my money back and things got really ugly—lots of shouting. When he caught hold of me to stop me packing I grabbed his precious school cricket bat and told him to take his hands off me and get out, or I'd hit him for six.'

Lucas threw back his head and laughed. 'And how big is this idiot?'

'Almost as tall as you, but heavier. Why?'

He shook his head in wonder. 'Emily, you can't be more than an inch or so over five feet, and delightfully rounded though you are I was able to carry you quite comfortably last night. Yet this prince among men actually turned tail when you threatened him?'

'He certainly did,' she said, her eyes glowing at the memory. 'I was dying to hit him and Miles knew it. So he did the sensible thing and took to his heels.'

Lucas laughed delightedly and ruffled her hair. 'Vicious creature. I'm thankful I don't own a cricket bat any more.'

Emily surveyed him, head on one side. 'Should the need arise I'd take more subtle revenge in your case.'

'You already have.' He laid a hand on his chest with a theatrical sigh. 'You've stolen my heart.'

'Very funny!' she jeered. 'Now go and lie on a sofa while I clear away. Then I'm going to attack your bedroom.'

Emily was putting the finishing touches to it when the doorbell rang. 'I'll get it,' she called, and went to open the door.

'Emily?' said Liz Donaldson in surprise. 'I didn't think you came here on Wednesdays.'

'She doesn't normally,' called Lucas from the living room door. 'Sorry to be inhospitable, Liz, but stay where you are. I might still be infectious.'

'So I gather. I got Emily's note, so I came to drop the paper in and see if you needed anything,' said Liz, who was tall and fair, with a bright-eyed, intelligent face. 'But if Lucas is infectious, why are you braving his germs, Emily?'

'I had flu not so long ago, with all the same side effects, so hopefully it's the same virus and I'm immune,' said Emily, desperately trying to hide her embarrassment. 'Did you have a good holiday? If Lucas will go back to his sofa you could come into the kitchen. I'll make coffee.'

'Can't stop, thanks,' said Liz with regret. 'So who's been looking after you, Lucas? Alice?'

'No. She's on holiday in Italy—and under orders to keep my state of health from my mother.' Lucas smiled blandly at Liz. 'My bug brought me home early last Friday, which was a stroke of luck because I met Emily in person for the first time. She's been an absolute saint: so worried because I had no one to soothe my fevered brow that she's dropped in from time to time to check on me.'

Liz wagged a finger at him. 'I hope you've doubled her wages!'

'Good God, no. Emily goes berserk at the mere mention of money.' He began to cough and Liz ordered him back to his sofa, promising to check on him later.

'It was very sweet of you to take care of Lucas, Emily,' she whispered, as she made for the door.

'Not at all.' Emily went outside with her on to the landing. 'Look, I'm sure the subject won't arise,' she said in an undertone, 'but if you happen to talk to Nat don't let on that I've been looking after Lucas, please.'

'I'm not going in today, but when I do, not a word, I promise.' Liz gave her a sparkling look. 'Would Nat be jealous, then?'

'Heavens no. But he might well rat on me to my brother!'

When Emily went back to Lucas he cast a dark look at her outdoor clothes.

'You really are going, then.'

'Yes, Lucas.'

'It's raining cats and dogs. Call a cab.'

'Certainly not. I enjoy the walk.'

He thrust a hand through his hair in frustration. 'You'll ruin that coat. If you must walk borrow something of mine. You'll be swamped, but at least you'll be dry.' He went into the bedroom and returned with a black ski-jacket and held it out.

'Oh, very well.' Secretly not at all keen to ruin the vintage velvet, Emily shrugged it off and slid her arms into the parka, tugging at the elasticated wristbands to free her hands. 'It comes down to my knees,' she said, pulling a face.

'Since you're so pig-headed about walking that's all to the good,' he said, his eyes softening at her ludicrous appearance.

'Thank you,' she said politely. 'Now. Remember to take your pills at regular intervals, Lucas, and wash them down with lots of water. There's a flask of lemon and honey on the counter, and cheese, eggs, bacon and cartons of soup in the fridge—'

'Strangely enough,' he said caustically, 'I managed my life quite well before you came into it.'

Emily blinked as though he'd slapped her face. And Lucas leapt to take her in his arms.

'I'm *sorry*. Don't cry. Please.'

'I'm not crying—just tired,' she said huskily, holding him off. 'Bye for now. I'll see you on Friday.'

'*Friday?*' He glared at her, incensed. 'Why not tomorrow?'

'I'm busy tomorrow.'

'Slaving away for your landlord, no doubt?'

'And for Mark.'

Lucas gazed down at her, his eyes locked on hers in such intense persuasion she turned her head away in self-defence. 'You could come here afterwards,' he coaxed. 'And stay the night.'

'I could,' she agreed, 'but I'm not going to. Goodbye, Lucas.'

His hot protest changed to a sudden paroxysm of coughing. 'You see?' he gasped, when he could speak. 'The mere thought of your absence, even for a day, and I'm heading for a relapse!'

Emily refused to be moved. 'You'll be fine.'

But the effort to tear herself away from Lucas left her in a mood which matched the miserable, sheeting rain as she hurried back to Spitalfields. The hooded jacket shielded her from the weather, but its warmth held a scent so exclusively Lucas that at one point Emily almost turned round and went back. Instead she kept going, determined on time to herself to think rationally about the future. Something she found impossible to do in Lucas Tennent's company.

When Emily let herself into Nat's house she hung the expensive padded jacket in the bathroom to dry, then unlocked her door and put away the food she'd bought on the way back. And at last checked her phone. But there was no message from Lucas, nor, to her relief, from Miles.

For once in her life Emily felt in need of a rest on her bed before opening her laptop to get down to work. She smiled a little. At least now she'd have a sizzler of a love scene to describe. Life with Miles had been so disappointing in that area she'd assumed the fault was hers. But Lucas had turned her preconceived idea about lovemaking on its head. Her eyes narrowed. Had that been *love*-making? Or just red-hot sex? Either way, it had been a revelation.

After spending almost an hour on her bed, something new to Emily in the daytime, she made herself some tea with the kettle that hid with a microwave and a tiny refrigerator on shelves behind a wicker screen. She kept basic supplies like tea and coffee in the cupboard underneath, but shopped as needed for anything more ambitious, and cooked it in Nat's kitchen during the day while he was out. But not today.

She took her tea over to the table used as a desk, plugged in the laptop, booted it up, and began to read over what she'd written so far. The tea cooled, forgotten beside her as she worked, but eventually she took a break and checked her watch, wondering if Lucas had remembered to take his medication. For heaven's sake, of course he has, she told herself crossly. But it was no use. With a sigh, she picked up the receiver and keyed in the number.

When an attractive—and unfamiliar—feminine voice answered, Emily disconnected hastily. Someone had obviously turned up at last to minister to the patient. Which, she informed herself savagely, was inevitable now he was better—and germ-free.

Furious at minding so much, Emily forced herself to forget Lucas and companion and settle down to work. And by the time she heard the evening noises of Nat and Mark getting home she'd made considerable progress. Pleased with herself, and suddenly hungry, she was filling rolls with cheese and salad greens when the phone rang. She waited, resigned, expecting Miles again, then tensed, her heart missing a beat when the message was from Lucas.

'Emily, I just rang to confirm that I've taken the pills, drunk pints of water and fruit juice and kept my coffee intake to a minimum. Ring back soon in awed approval—'

'I'm here,' she interrupted breathlessly. 'How do you feel?'

'Lonely.'

Emily scowled in silence.

'I know you rang earlier on,' he went on. 'You forgot to cover your electronic tracks. That was Caroline who answered, by the way.'

Caroline. His assistant! Emily revived. 'Did she remind you to take your pill?'

'You could have asked her yourself if you hadn't rung off. But Caroline came to deliver messages and talk work, not pills. And, wary of my germs, she cleared off as soon as she could. What are you doing right now?' he added abruptly.

'Nothing. I've just closed the laptop after a session on the Great Work, and now I'm going to eat something. I trust you are, too?'

'Yes, Nurse. Rather to my surprise, I'm quite hungry. Liz called back this afternoon with some kind of casserole I can heat in the microwave.'

'So I don't have to worry any more.'

'Were you worried?'

'The night you had a cough like a chainsaw, yes, I was. Bloodshot eyes apart, you looked a bit lacking in the red corpuscle department, too.'

He laughed. 'Half-dead I may have been, but I soon came back to life under your care, Emily.'

Her cheeks flamed at the memory. 'Then please don't waste my efforts. Keep taking the tablets.'

'It's going to be a long day tomorrow without you, Emily,' he said, in a tone which badly undermined her famous resolutions.

'Catch up on all the reading you never have time for,' she advised briskly. 'Goodnight, sleep well.' Emily put the phone down quickly, in case Lucas began persuading her to spend time with him the next day. And in case she said yes.

Emily rang her mother later, to report that she'd survived Lucas Tennent's flu unscathed—news received with much relief by her mother, who went on to fire off several barbed questions about vitamins and sensible eating before passing on Richard Warner's love to his daughter and concluding with her own. To Emily's relief, there wasn't a word about Miles.

But when she rang Ginny later, her friend was plainly worried to hear that Miles was still leaving messages.

'What on earth does he want? You didn't make off with his family silver, or something?'

'And me a vicar's daughter? Certainly not.'

'So how did it go with the gorgeous patient?'

'*Im*patient, you mean. As invalids go, he's the end.'

'Is he grateful to you?'

'Yes. Now he's better, anyway. He was very ill at one stage. I had to call a doctor.'

'Wow. He must have been pretty bad to want that.'

'Lucas didn't want it at all. Made a huge fuss. Fortunately his sister rang, read him the riot act, and asked me to arrange it.' Emily chuckled evilly. 'You should have seen his face when a woman doctor arrived.'

They went on chatting for a while, as they always did, before Ginny came to a halt because Charlie was due home. 'Emily,' she said, suddenly serious. 'You're all right, are you? Really, I mean?'

'Absolutely fine. Not a cough or a sneeze to my name.'

'I don't mean that.' Ginny hesitated. 'What I'm trying to say, with my usual consummate tact, is that you've just got over the break-up with Miles. So don't do anything reckless, Em. Please.'

Too late for warnings of that kind, thought Emily afterwards. Reckless didn't begin to describe her behaviour with Lucas Tennent. She should have resisted, protested, done *something*. But, from the moment he'd seized her in his arms, the warning signals from her brain had never had a chance. Besides, if she had put a stop to it all she might have gone through life with no experience of what sublime, earthy magic the act of love could actually be. She shivered at the memory. And didn't blame Lucas in the slightest, whatever the outcome. He hadn't asked her to come running to play nurse. A wry little smile played at the corners of her mouth and her eyes grew dreamy. There was no point in wasting time on regrets over an experience Lucas had described very aptly as miraculous.

Emily came back to earth with a bump. In future, she would avoid all contact with miracles and confine her charitable impulses to putting coins in collection boxes.

Time hung heavy for Emily for the rest of the evening. She felt too tired to open up her laptop, yet too restless to read. In the act of pouring boiling water on a teabag, she was seized by a sudden rush of panic and put the kettle down with an unsteady hand. It was imperative that she found *some* way to occupy her mind. Her cleaning jobs conveniently left her mind free to compose drafts for her novel, but they also left it free to worry about what fate had, or didn't have, in store for her.

CHAPTER EIGHT

THE following morning the phone rang in Nat's kitchen while Emily was finishing her usual cleaning routine. She went on mopping the floor, leaving the machine to pick up as usual, then looked up, her attention caught, when the message began.

'Nat, this is Louise Powell. I don't have your office number, or your mobile, and I don't like to ask Thea, but I thought you ought to know that she's ill—'

'Louise,' Emily broke in. 'This is Emily Warner. What's wrong? Can I help?'

'Emily?' said Louise, surprised, but too worried to ask questions. 'Can you possibly contact Nat for me? Thea just passed out on the kitchen floor. I've got her to bed now, but she looks absolutely ghastly.'

'Heavens, Louise, have you contacted her mother?'

'Away on a cruise. Always the way, isn't it? I've rung the doctor, and I can fetch Tom and Lucy from school this afternoon with my lot, and feed them, too, of course. Only too glad to help. But if you can get in touch with Nat I'd be terribly grateful.'

'I'll ring him straight away,' Emily assured her. 'Don't worry, Louise. I'll find him. Give me your number so I can let you know what's happening.'

To Emily's frustration, Nat's cellphone was switched off. She rang his firm's number, learned he was in an important meeting, and asked to speak to Mrs Donaldson instead.

'Right,' said Liz crisply, when Emily explained. 'I'll

haul Nat out at once. This is just the chance he needs. He can rush to Thea's bedside like a knight in shining armour. Perfect. Don't worry, Emily, I'll barge in there and get him to ring you back right away.'

'Bless you, Liz.'

Emily raced up the two steep flights of stairs to her own room just in time to answer the phone to a frantic Nat Sedley.

'Emily, for God's sake tell me what's wrong? Is Thea in hospital—?'

'No, nothing like that.' Breathless, Emily passed on the message and the phone number, assuring him that Louise Powell had promised to pick Tom and Lucy up after school.

'Right,' said Nat tersely. 'I'll ring Louise, then I'm off. I'll drive straight from here. Thanks a lot, Emily. I'll ring you tonight to keep you up to speed.'

Emily glared at the red light which had been winking on her phone throughout her conversation with Nat. Life had been so much simpler before the answer-machine her parents had insisted on. Refusing to pander to it, she made herself a cup of coffee and drank half of it before pressing the button.

'Emily, you haven't rung to ask how I am,' said a hoarse, aggrieved voice. 'In case you're interested, I passed a very restless night without you. I miss you.'

Emily reached out a hand to ring Lucas back, then changed her mind. She would be seeing him tomorrow. He could wait until then. Or rather, she could. Somehow.

After lunch, her cleaning sessions over, Emily opened her laptop and settled down to work. She took a deep breath and plunged into the love-scene, embarrassed to find her face hot and her pulse racing as she painted a verbal picture of the bliss experienced in Lucas

Tennent's arms. Her fingers flew over the keys as though possessed, then she stopped, groaning in frustration. She'd used his name. 'James,' she said through her teeth. 'The man's name is James, not Lucas.' She went back over the scene, so involved in the changes that she answered the phone without thinking.

'Success at last!' said a triumphant voice, but Emily slammed the phone down, waited until it rang again, and listened, resigned, while Miles began leaving a furious message.

'Answer me, God dammit. What the hell are you playing at, Emily? I just want my property back. So ring me. Now.'

Emily stared at the phone, mystified. What property? In her frantic hurry to get out of the flat she'd been forced to leave some of her own things behind, let alone make off with anything belonging to Miles.

To get some peace, Emily took the receiver off and put it on the table beside her so she could work undisturbed. And only put it back later because Nat was due to ring some time.

When it rang almost immediately, Emily seized it eagerly. 'Nat?'

'Sorry to disappoint you,' snapped a hostile voice.

'Oh.' She bit her lip. 'Hello, Lucas. How are you?'

'If it's of any interest, I feel better. Not wonderful. But better. I left a message earlier.'

'I know. I didn't ring back because—'

'Because you were waiting to hear from your landlord.'

'No.' Emily was silent for a moment. 'I had a quite different reason.'

'What is it?'

'I'd hate you to think I was taking advantage of—of our relationship because of what happened that night.'

'Ah. So you do admit we have a relationship,' he said triumphantly.

'I should have said arrangement. You the employer, me the cleaner.'

'Emily,' he said, his voice dangerously quiet. 'It's a good thing you're not here with me right now, or I'd wring your pretty little neck.'

'In that case,' she said lightly, 'I'd better not come to your place tomorrow.'

'If you don't, I'll leave my sickbed to fetch you.'

'You don't know my address.'

'Liz gave it to me.'

'You *asked* her for it?'

'Damn right I did.' Lucas's laugh sent trickles down her spine. 'She nobly refrained from asking why I needed it, tactful lady. But be warned, Emily, I know where you live.'

'Is that a threat?' she demanded.

'Just making sure you turn up tomorrow. As promised,' he said significantly. 'Goodnight. Sleep well.'

Emily was in bed when Nat rang with an apology for calling so late.

Thea, he reported, had been trying to fight off flu with over-the-counter medication in an effort to keep going for the twins. The faint had been the inevitable result of lack of food coupled with sleepless nights.

'How is she now?'

'Running a temperature, and so wretched, poor darling, she gave in without a word when I laid the law down about staying to take care of her, *and* my children.'

'You know, Nat, I'm sorry Thea's ill,' said Emily thoughtfully, 'but in other ways—'

'It's an ill wind, and so on,' he finished for her. 'One snag, though, Emily. Louise Powell told her you answered my phone today.'

'Only because I was mopping your kitchen floor, Mr Sedley!'

'Thea didn't know that, obviously. But apparently Tom and Lucy could talk about nothing else but you when they went back after half-term, so my wife asked me point blank if there was anything between you and me now, Emily.'

'*What?* I hope you convinced her that's utter nonsense, Nat Sedley.'

'Yes. In the end,' he said, an odd note in his voice. 'But only at the cost of a little white lie.'

Emily braced herself. 'What kind?'

'I was so determined to clear the decks with Thea that I said you were passionately in love with the new man in your life.'

'Thanks a bunch!'

'Don't worry. You don't have to produce him in the flesh. But I'd like our stories to match if you happen to talk to Thea.'

'Right.' Emily hesitated. 'Nat, what about the original problem? Is Thea coming round on that one, too?'

'Yes, thank God. We had a long talk this evening, after I put a jubilant pair of twins to bed. Let's just say I'll go happy to bed myself tonight.'

Wishing she could say the same, Emily spent a restless night, gave up trying to sleep at last, and with the aim of getting finished to be with Lucas as soon as she could, arrived so early at the Donaldsons' flat that Liz hadn't left for work.

'Goodness, you're an early bird, Emily,' she said, surprised. 'Ben's only just left. I'm agog to know what happened with Nat, so shoot. You won't be telling tales out of school,' she added, when Emily looked troubled. 'At the firm, all Nat's colleagues know the story. Besides, I've met Thea, even been to a party at their house in Chastlecombe. How is she?'

Emily explained the situation and passed on the news that Nat was staying on to look after his wife and children.

'But that's wonderful.' Liz raised an eyebrow. 'Why aren't you happy about it?'

'Because the original rift may be healed, but Thea's now got some crazy idea that Nat's interested in me, for heaven's sake.' Emily groaned in despair. 'And to convince her otherwise he told her I'm having a red-hot affair with someone else.'

Liz gave a shout of laughter. 'Poor Thea. She's almost pathologically jealous where Nat is concerned. Which is understandable. Thea's a honey, a wonderful homemaker and a brilliant mother. But pretty she's not. And Nat is quite the handsomest man I've ever laid eyes on. Don't let on to Ben I said that,' she added, laughing.

'I won't.' Emily hesitated. 'Look, Liz, I suppose I shouldn't be asking this, but do you know if Thea ever had reason to be jealous of Nat?'

'Absolutely not,' Liz assured her. 'The trouble started when Nat's PA left. Enter Melanie Baker—blonde hair, long legs and cleavage. She lusted after Nat from the first, but he wasn't having any. So when they worked late together one night Melanie tried to seduce him.'

'Wow! What did Nat do?'

'Promptly dispensed with her services. Whereupon Melanie, spitting fire, storms down to Chastlecombe and tells Thea she's been having a sizzling affair with Nat from the day they met. Sweet, unremarkable Thea took one look at this centrefold blonde and believed every word.'

'Instead of trusting her husband. Poor Thea. Anyway,' added Emily, brightening, 'according to Nat, everything's fine now, except for her crazy idea that he fancies me, of all people.'

'Not so crazy, Emily,' said Liz, getting up. 'You're attractive and female and you live in Nat's house—you know what they say about propinquity.'

'I assure you it doesn't apply in this case. Besides, Thea ought to know me better than that—' Emily was struck by a sudden thought. 'Oh, crikey. Once she's better, I hope she doesn't turn up on spec in Spitalfields to meet this lover Nat dreamed up for me.'

'If she does, there must be someone you can trot out for the purpose?' Liz grinned. 'I'd offer Ben for the role, but Thea's met him.'

After Liz left, Emily worked faster than usual in her hurry to see Lucas. When she was sure the flat was immaculate, she locked up and ran across the cobbled street to the converted eighteenth-century warehouse she much preferred to the modern apartment block which housed the Donaldsons.

Strange, she thought, as she went up in the lift. After spending her childhood in a draughty Victorian vicarage she'd yearned for something modern and labour-saving when she went flat-hunting with Ginny. The one they'd rented was a bit poky, or bijou in brochure speak. But Emily had loved it so much it had taken endless persuasion from Miles to coax her to leave it for the bigger, pricier apartment of his own choice.

But now she'd regressed a couple of centuries in her taste, both in Nat's house in Spitalfields and in Lucas's home, which, though a hip loft conversion, was part of an old, historic building. She loved both places. Which was silly when neither would feature permanently in her life. In fact, thought Emily gloomily, she would be forced to look for pastures new right away if Thea intended spending much time with Nat in London.

Before Emily could put the key in the lock Lucas opened the door, dressed in a Cambridge-blue sweater and vintage jeans. He looked very different from the irritable invalid of only days before.

'I heard the lift.' He smiled as he took the borrowed ski-jacket she held out. 'Hello, Emily.'

'Hi,' she said breathlessly. 'How do you feel?'

'All the better for seeing you,' he said softly, with a look in his eye which did serious damage to her resolutions. 'I missed you.'

'It's only been a couple of days,' she said, brushing past him to take off her jacket, but he was too quick for her and slid it from her shoulders.

'It felt a hell of a sight longer than that!' His lips twitched. 'Relax. I won't remove anything else.'

She ignored him and went off to the kitchen. 'If you'll sit in the living room I'll leave it until last,' she said briskly.

'Let's have coffee first.' He seized her waist and sat her on one of the stools at the bar. 'Like me, it's ready and waiting for you.'

This, thought Emily bitterly, wasn't fair.

Lucas slid on to the stool beside her and filled two mugs. 'There. While you drink that tell me everything you've done since I saw you last.' He gave her a challenging look. 'I presume you're still getting messages from Miles?'

'Why do you think that?' she asked, surprised.

'Because every time I ring the machine takes over for a while before you answer.' Lucas took her hand and stroked a finger over it. 'Tell me. Is that bastard frightening you?'

Not half as much as you are, thought Emily, panicking. 'He says I've made off with something belonging to him.'

'And have you?'

She shrugged. 'The only thing I can think of is the laptop. I gave it to him for his birthday, I admit. But I paid for it and still have the receipt to prove it, so he's out of luck if he wants it back.'

'If that's all he wants, give him the damn thing,' said Lucas irritably. 'I'll buy you another one.'

'Certainly not.' Emily detached her hand. 'Anyway, I'm not worried about Miles.'

'Then what's wrong? Tell me.'

'I can't,' she said, depressed. 'Most of it is none of my business.'

'But it's worrying the hell out of you, so get it off your chest. Or do you have to rush back to Spitalfields to minister to your landlord?' He grinned when she glared at him, then sobered. 'Seriously, Emily, come and sit down for a while and tell me what's wrong. You can trust me to keep it to myself, whatever it is.'

'I know that.'

When they were installed at opposite ends of the familiar sofa, Emily gave Lucas a brief outline of the trouble between Nat and Thea Sedley, and how the latter's illness had been the catalyst to bring them back together.

'Amazing thing, influenza,' commented Lucas. 'Without it, you and I might never have met, and in the Sedleys' case it's mended a broken marriage. I assume it is mended now?' he added.

'More or less.' Not without reluctance, Emily told him about Thea's suspicions where she was concerned.

'Can't say I blame her there,' said Lucas, looking down his nose. 'I share her point of view.'

'But you don't know Nat, whereas Thea's known *me* all my life.' Emily thrust her hair behind her ears in agitation. 'I would never dream of doing anything to harm her—or the twins.'

Lucas moved nearer to take her hand again. 'Emily, I refuse to believe your money was the only attraction for Miles. And you know damn well *I* don't find you a turn-off either. Thea Sedley obviously thinks her husband feels the same.'

'She doesn't any more,' said Emily gloomily. 'Nat's told her I'm violently in love with the new man in my life.'

'And who the devil's that?' he demanded, eyes slitted.

She shook his hand off impatiently. 'A phantom lover who doesn't exist.'

'Ah.' Lucas relaxed. 'So what happens if the suspicious Mrs Sedley turns up unexpectedly one day, thirsting for an introduction?'

'Lord knows,' said Emily despondently. 'Liz would have offered Ben's services, but unfortunately Thea knows him.'

'She doesn't know me.'

'It's no joking matter,' she snapped.

'Who's joking?'

Emily stared at him, startled.

'I mean it,' said Lucas casually. 'If the occasion arises I'd be happy to oblige. After all, there's no lie involved.' He touched a hand to her cheek. 'On one recent, unforgettable occasion I actually was your lover.'

Emily sprang up precipitately. 'Time I made a start,' she blurted.

For the next two hours Emily cleaned and polished and scoured, ignoring Lucas's frequent demands that she take a break, or stop altogether.

In the end he seized his state-of-the-art vacuum cleaner and thrust it in a kitchen cupboard. 'Stop it right now,' he said in a tone which brooked no argument. 'Or are you by any chance trying to solve our little problem by sheer physical exertion?'

She thrust damp hair from her forehead, her eyes widening as she realised what he meant. 'Are you serious?'

'It occurred to me,' he said grimly.

'Well, it didn't occur to me!' she spat at him. 'I was merely trying to get everything done as quickly as possible so I could get back where I belong.'

Lucas raised an eyebrow. 'After what you've told me about his wife, do you feel you belong in Sedley's house any more?'

Emily stared at him, stricken. 'No—I suppose I don't. I'd better start looking for somewhere else.' She glanced at her watch. 'It's past two. Shouldn't you be taking some medication?'

'In a minute. Let's have some lunch.'

'But I didn't do any shopping on the way in,' she reminded him, seized by the sudden urge to throw herself into Lucas Tennent's arms and cry her eyes out. Which was idiotic. There was nothing to cry about. She just needed sleep. 'Shall I dash out for something now?'

'Certainly not. I ordered in. For the moment you're going nowhere,' he said inexorably. 'Wash your hands, or whatever, then come and eat.'

When Emily got back from the bathroom she found a tray waiting on the chest in front of the familiar sofa.

'Not exactly a feast,' Lucas said, indicating the platter of sandwiches. 'But I thought the occasion merited a touch of ceremony.' He set this thumbs to the cork of a bottle of champagne, removed it neatly, then filled a couple of tulip-shaped glasses and handed one to her.

Emily took it with a dazed word of thanks, then followed his beckoning hand and sat beside him on the sofa. 'Champagne? What are we celebrating? Your recovery from flu, or is it your birthday?'

'Something far more important—an anniversary.' He touched his glass to hers. 'It's exactly a week, almost to the minute, since you and I met for the first time.'

Emily almost dropped the glass.

Lucas grinned. 'It's only a sandwich and a glass of bubbly, woman. And in broad daylight in the afternoon, at that. Hardly cause for panic.'

'I'm not panicking,' she lied, and gulped down some champagne. 'These look delicious,' she added brightly when Lucas handed her a filled plate.

'I would have preferred to take you out to dinner, but I thought you might lay down the law about behaving sensibly—'

'I certainly would!'

'I meant,' said Lucas, 'that you'd rage about relapses and so on. So we'll postpone the dinner date until you think the time is right.'

'Lucas,' said Emily patiently. 'This is lovely, and I'm flattered you went to so much trouble, but that's as far as it goes. I'm certainly not dining out with you.'

'Why not? It's just a way of saying thanks for all you've done for me,' he said, undeterred. 'Nothing more sinister than that.'

Surprised to find the argument had sharpened her appetite, Emily started on another sandwich and prepared

to do battle. 'Pointless rather than sinister, Lucas. Because when you're fit and well, and back in the City,
things will revert to normal between us. You the City
Banker, me your cleaner. And never the twain shall meet
and all that.'

'I thought we'd put paid to all that nonsense.' Lucas
pushed his plate away and refilled their glasses. 'Are you
by any chance a snob, Emily Warner?'

She stared at him in exasperation and waved a hand
around. 'How do you work that out? You own this. I
live in one room I rent for such a small amount it's
tantamount to charity. How can I possibly be a snob?'

'Inverted variety.' He raised a sardonic eyebrow.
'Does Mrs Sedley know how little you pay for your
room, by the way?'

Emily sniffed. 'I've no idea.' She drained her glass
recklessly. 'You know,' she said, with a confiding air
fostered by the champagne, 'it really hacked me off to
think that Thea suspected me of—of—'

'Sharing her husband's bed?'

'I don't suppose she went that far!' Emily shrugged.
'If so, it's utterly ridiculous. I don't think of Nat that
way.'

Lucas topped up her glass. 'If she's jealous of him, I
take it Sedley's got a lot going for him in the looks
department.'

'Liz says he's the handsomest man she's ever met.'
Emily thought for a bit. 'How are you on movie stars?'

'Adequate.'

'Think of a young Robert Redford, only taller and
even better-looking, if that's possible.'

'Good God!' Lucas eyed her askance. 'And you don't
find Sedley attractive?'

'Of course I do, but not in the way you mean. Nat's

kind and nice and I like him a lot. I'm grateful to him, too. But to me he's just my brother's friend and not my type at all. I don't go for fair men.'

'In that case—' Without warning, he scooped her on to his lap and kissed her. 'Part of the celebration,' he whispered against her parted lips. 'If this is never going to happen again you can at least agree to a few kisses.'

'Because of your outlay on champagne?' she said rashly, and said no more for some time, returning kisses that grew so heated it was alarmingly obvious where they would lead if she didn't do something fast. But when Emily gathered her wine-blunted wits about her and tried to get free, Lucas held her tightly against his chest.

'I want you, Emily,' he said hoarsely.

'No!' She shook her head frantically. 'It's not going to happen again, Lucas.'

He tipped her face up to his. 'You don't want me?'

'No,' she lied in desperation. 'I don't.'

'You mean that?' he demanded.

'Yes,' she said woodenly, and his eyes hardened, the heat in them icing over so quickly she shivered and scrambled to her feet. She ran into the kitchen, almost tripping over her bag in her hurry to be gone.

'Wait,' said Lucas, catching her up in the hall. 'There's still a certain matter outstanding between us. Or have you forgotten?'

'Are you serious?' Emily threw him a scornful look. 'I never forget it for an instant, believe me.' She snatched up her coat, disdaining his help as she pulled it on. 'Certainly not enough to risk the same mistake twice.' She grabbed her backpack by the straps and made for the door, but Lucas stood barring her way.

'Emily. Please. If you find somewhere else to live let me know.'

'All right.' Her mouth dropped. 'Though, in the interests of the Sedley marriage, perhaps I'd better stay where I am for the time being after all. Otherwise, Thea might think her suspicions were right.' She looked up with a bright smile. 'Remember to finish the entire course of tablets, Lucas. You're obviously a lot better—'

'I'm glad you think so,' he said grimly, then took her hand. 'Have a good rest this weekend, Emily. I'll see you on Monday.'

She shook her head. 'No, Lucas. I'll wait until you start work again before I come back to clean. I'm sure you can manage until then. Unless you'd rather get someone else—'

'I don't want anyone else,' he said through his teeth. 'I want you.'

Emily gave him a despairing look and hurried out on to the landing outside the flat, feeling oddly hurt when Lucas closed his door before she even got into the lift.

Outside in the windy, cobbled street, Emily found that the champagne had given her a splitting headache and the straps of her backpack were cutting into her shoulders for once. And she was halfway back to Spitalfields before she remembered that Lucas hadn't given her the usual Friday cheque.

CHAPTER NINE

'FOR heaven's sake, Emily, you look terrible,' said Ginny, when they met as usual the next day. 'Are you in mourning, or something?'

To match her mood, Emily was wearing unrelieved black, the only touch of colour her eyes and a lipstick so bright she rarely used it on the mouth she considered too full for bright shades. 'I'm tired, that's all.'

'You're sure you haven't caught this man's flu?'

'Yes. It's just lack of sleep.'

'So what's keeping you awake at night?'

Not even to Ginny could Emily confide the real reason for her insomnia. Instead, she told her friend about Nat and Thea and the phantom lover.

Ginny chuckled as she dished out coffee and buns and gave Emily the gooiest. 'You look as though you could do with it. Are you eating properly?'

'Yes, Mummy!' Emily tucked into her cake, feeling better, as always, in Ginny's company. 'How's Charlie?'

'At a conference this weekend. At least, that's what he tells me.'

'Come off it,' jeered Emily. 'You know perfectly well Charlie's never looked at another woman since the day he met you.'

'Of course I do,' said Ginny fondly. 'This all came up unexpectedly. He had to take someone else's place. So how about coming round to our place to keep me company tonight? We can get a bottle of wine and a video and be all girly.'

Emily gave a fleeting thought to the work she'd meant to do on her novel over the weekend, but the prospect of a day away from her lonely room—and her telephone—was too tempting to pass up. 'I'd like that a lot.'

Emily slept better on Ginny's sofabed than she had for some time, and returned to Spitalfields late the following afternoon, surprised to find no messages for once. Her immediate reaction was sharp disappointment because Lucas hadn't rung, followed by relief because Miles hadn't either. Emily put out a hand to ring Lucas, then changed her mind and opened the laptop instead. She would recycle her emotions by transferring them to the central female character in her novel.

Next morning, Emily was on her way out of the Donaldsons' flat when the bell rang. When she opened the door as far as the safety-chain allowed, her heart skipped a beat at the sight of Lucas.

'Let me in, Emily.'

She took the chain off and turned away to pick up her bag. 'I'm just leaving.'

'I was afraid I'd missed you.' He stood just inside the door, looming large in the padded jacket. 'How are you?'

'Fine. How are you?'

'Only a few more antibiotics to go. I'll be back in work soon.'

'That's good.'

Silence fell, loud with things unsaid.

'Look, it's too soon for me to know yet, Lucas,' said Emily, cutting straight to the chase. 'I promised to let you know and I will.' She gave him a wry little smile.

'My father's a clergyman, remember. He brought me up to keep my promises.'

'Admirable habit,' said Lucas, relieving her of the backpack. 'I never knew my father.'

Emily's eyes softened. 'He died when you were little?'

'No. When Ally and I were small he just left home one day and never came back.'

She gazed at him in horror. 'Why?'

'When my mother thought we were old enough to understand, she told us he was a free spirit who felt stifled by marriage and fatherhood.' His jaw clenched. 'She was wrong.'

'About your father?'

'About me. I'll never understand how a man could do that. Just take off and slough off his responsibilities like so much unwanted baggage.' Lucas paused. 'Look, if you've finished here have some coffee at my place before you go back, Emily.'

'All right.' She made sure the door was locked behind them and followed Lucas into the lift.

'I rang you over the weekend,' he informed her.

'You didn't leave a message.'

'The idea was to speak to you, not to a machine.'

'I was with the friend I used to live with. Ginny and I still meet every Saturday morning, but this weekend her husband was away so I stayed the night with her. Though I don't know why I'm telling you this,' she added with sudden irritability. 'I don't have to report to you.'

Lucas smiled faintly as they reached the ground floor. 'True. But I was worried when I couldn't reach you.'

'Why?' she demanded, shivering in the wind which

funnelled down the street as they crossed the cobbles to his building.

'I was afraid you'd succumbed to my flu after all.'

'In which case, I would have been in my room.'

'You could have gone home to your mother for more cosseting.'

She shook her head. 'I'm keeping well away from Chastlecombe for the time being.'

The lift in the converted warehouse was bigger than in the modern building next door, but even so Emily felt hot and bothered by the time they reached the top floor. In such close proximity to Lucas every hormone she possessed clamoured in response to the warmth from his body and the familiar tang of the soap he used mingled with the clean male scent of his skin. When they went into his flat he dumped her bag down, shed his jacket and took her raincoat, as though they'd done this a hundred times before, then followed her into the kitchen.

'Shall I make the coffee?' offered Emily.

'If you like.' He gave her a straight look. 'I take it you're here with me solely out of pity about my defecting father?'

'Sympathy, not pity.' Which wasn't the exact truth. She'd come with him because she wanted—needed—to be with him, if only for a little while, before going back to her solitary room.

Lucas sat on a stool and leaned his elbows on the counter to watch her get to grips with the coffee-machine. 'Normally, I never discuss my father. But I told *you* the story, Emily, to make a point. Well, two points, actually.'

Emily threw him a curious look as she took porcelain mugs from a cupboard. 'Which are?'

'First of all, it seemed a good idea to kill this bee in your bonnet about the social difference between us. I'm well-educated, I admit, but that's because I've always worked hard and I've been lucky enough to win scholarships at the necessary stages. And these days I'm successful in my career. But you fell asleep on me the other night so I didn't tell the whole story. Unlike you, Emily Warner, I'm the product of a single parent family. When my father abandoned us we moved in with my grandmother and Mother had to go back to work to feed and clothe us.'

Emily gazed at him in horrified sympathy as she passed him his coffee. 'What did she do?'

'She'd been a legal secretary before her marriage, but to earn money straight away she worked in a shop before she finally landed a job with the local solicitor.' Lucas's mouth twisted. 'Ally and I used to cry for our father in the beginning, but in the way of the young we eventually forgot him. I was in my first year in grammar school before the lack of a dad was really brought home to me. Schoolboys can be cruel young savages.'

'Did your father ever come back?' said Emily.

'No. In true beachcombing fashion his free spirit eventually took him to a Pacific island so small and remote it took months for news of his death to reach my mother.'

'After all that time was she upset?'

'Inconsolable for a while.' His eyes hardened. 'She'd never stopped loving him.'

Emily finished her coffee, at a loss for something to say. Even on acquaintance as short as theirs, she knew that baring his soul was hard for Lucas Tennent. He would probably curse himself for it afterwards. Maybe her, too.

'I had another reason for telling you,' he informed her, picking up on her reaction. 'If you are expecting my baby, Emily, you can be sure I won't evade *my* responsibilities. No child of mine will grow up without knowing his father.'

'That's very high-minded and noble,' she commented after a pause. 'Doesn't the mother—me, in this particular instance—have a say in this?'

Lucas's eyes flickered in surprise. 'Well, yes, of course. But surely you want my support if the worst happens?'

Emily's unruly heart contracted painfully. She looked at her watch. 'Time I was off. Let me know when you go back to work and I'll come and sort this place out for you. Unless you'd rather find another cleaner—'

'To hell with the cleaning! We need to talk about the necessary arrangements if you're pregnant, woman,' he growled, intercepting her as she passed him.

'Let's leave all that until I know whether the *worst* has actually happened,' she flung at him. 'Goodbye, Lucas.'

'Emily,' he said, striding after her as she made for the door. 'I put it badly—'

'But *so* accurately. My sentiments, exactly.' Emily turned her back on him and got in the lift she was beginning to dislike, because lately she so often went down in it feeling utterly miserable.

When she got back, Emily was surprised to find Nat in the hall as she let herself in.

'I'm on a flying visit. Louise Powell's with Thea,' he

explained. 'She'll fetch the twins and stay with Thea until I get back. My presence is required at a meeting this afternoon, then I'll come here afterwards for some clothes and go back to Chastlecombe for the rest of the week.'

'How is Thea?'

'Better, but still pretty fragile, poor darling.' Nat's grin took ten years off him. 'But with my tender loving care she'll soon be right as rain.'

'I'd send her my love, but I'm not top of Thea's list at the moment,' said Emily glumly.

'Actually, she's come round on that subject now, even begged me not to tell you she'd been so silly.'

Emily brightened. 'I'm off the hook, then?'

'Not exactly. She's still asking for details of this dream lover of yours.' Nat grinned widely. 'I was pretty unimaginative—tall, dark and handsome was all I could come up with. Must run—see you later.'

Emily trudged up the stairs to her room, cheering up a little when there were no messages waiting for her. Miles had obviously given up.

With no need to clean for Nat that day, Emily decided to skip lunch until she'd done Mark's rooms, and put in a couple of hours before retreating upstairs for a shower. Afterwards, comfortable in pull-on pink jersey trousers and black cable sweater, Emily made a sandwich and drank some tea. While she'd been cleaning, thoughts of Lucas kept coming between her and the next instalment, but now, she ordered herself, opening the laptop, she would banish him by getting to grips with her story. She spent a long time editing what she'd written, then started on the next chapter. For a long time her absorption was fierce, but eventually it dawned on her that there was something going on downstairs. Emily opened her door to hear familiar voices raised in altercation in the hall far below, and flew, barefoot, down two flights of stairs, skidding to a halt in the hall when two male faces swivelled towards her; Nat's deeply embarrassed, the other rigid with offence.

'A slight misunderstanding, Em,' explained Nat. 'I've just tried to throw your visitor out. From your description I thought he was Miles Denny.'

'I'd better introduce you,' said Emily, her spirits rising so precipitously that she smiled brilliantly on both men. 'Nat, this is Liz's friend, Lucas Tennent, one of the people I clean for. As you've probably guessed, Lucas, this is Nat Sedley, my landlord.'

The two men eyed each other warily, then Nat's face broke into an apologetic grin as he held out his hand to Lucas. 'Humble apologies! A case of mistaken identity. Emily's brother gave me strict instructions to throw the ex-boyfriend out if he showed his face here.'

To Emily's relief, Lucas grinned back as he shifted a sheaf of flowers to the hand holding a carrier-bag so he could shake Nat's. 'No harm done. The flowers suffered the most.'

'Are they for me?' said Emily idiotically.

'Who else?' said Lucas, and thrust them at her. 'Perhaps you can salvage some of them.'

Nat's vivid blue eyes moved from one face to the other with interest. 'Look, I'm just off to Gloucestershire, so I haven't got time to give you a whisky by way of apology, but Emily can do that. She knows where I keep the drinks. Make yourself at home in my place, if you like—not, I assure you, that I object to gentleman callers in Emily's room.' He glanced at his watch and whistled. 'I'm late. Promised to be home by bathtime. See you.'

He grabbed a suitcase and went out at a run, leaving a tense silence behind him after he closed his elegant front door.

'Do you get many?' asked Lucas eventually.

'Flowers?'

'Callers.'

Emily shook her head. 'You're the first.'

Another silence.

'So what do we do now?' he asked. 'Do you want me to go?'

She looked down at the flowers. 'I'd better put these in water. Would you like that whisky Nat mentioned?'

'Damn right I would.' He smiled crookedly. 'It's not every day of the week I get mugged.'

Emily chuckled. 'I don't see a black eye.'

'No, fortunately. And it only got as far as it did because Sedley took me by surprise. I didn't anticipate ejection into the street the minute I mentioned your name!'

She smiled ruefully. 'Sorry about that. Nat's never met Miles. I just gave him a description.'

'Which obviously fitted me down to the ground.'

'Not really. You're both tall, dark and very—' She halted.

'Go on!'

'In Miles's case, very full of himself.'

Lucas looked offended. 'And is that how you see *me*?'

'No. Confident, maybe? Self-assured?'

'Better,' he conceded grudgingly. 'And is Miles prettier than me?'

'Heavens, no. You win by a length in the looks department.' She showed him into Nat's small, elegant drawing-room. 'If you'll wait here for a moment I'll just put these in water.'

Emily hurried along the hall to Nat's kitchen, thrust the sheaf of spring flowers into the kitchen sink, half-filled it with water, then rejoined Lucas, who was taking in his surroundings with interest.

'Your landlord has great taste,' he told her, then frowned as his eyes dropped to her feet. 'Shouldn't you be wearing shoes?'

'When I heard the fracas I ran down as I was.' Emily hesitated. 'Look, it was very kind of Nat to offer the use of his place, but—'

'You'd rather I left.'

'No,' she said impatiently. 'I didn't mean that at all. I don't have any whisky, but I can offer you some reasonable wine. Though you'll have to come up to my room to share it. Don't worry,' she added. 'My mother provided me with a chair comfortable enough for you to sit in.'

'I'm delighted.' He grinned. 'Are you all right without shoes, or shall I carry you up?'

'In your state of health?' she jeered. 'Be warned. These are serious stairs—two flights of them, and murderously steep.'

'Stairway to heaven,' he said promptly. 'If your room's at the top.'

'Corny!' Emily wrinkled her nose at him, then started up the stairs with a practised speed which had Lucas coughing by the time they reached the landing outside her room.

'Holy Moses!' he gasped. 'This place could do with a lift.'

'Inharmonious with early Georgian architecture,' she said loftily, and went through her open door, beckoning Lucas inside. 'Welcome to my eyrie.'

Like the rest of the house, the room was high-ceilinged, with beautiful plasterwork picked out in white against walls painted pale, authentic green.

Looking at the room as though he meant to memorise it, Lucas stood in the doorway, carrier-bag in hand, while Emily closed down her laptop, burningly aware of his physical presence. In black jeans and a brown leather windbreaker well-worn enough to match the bigger chair, he dominated her private space to such an extent she wished they'd stayed downstairs in Nat's place.

'Great room,' he said at last. 'Your taste in furnishing or Sedley's?'

'The paintwork had been done and the bed and ward-robe were already *in situ*. But Andy donated the chair and table I use as a work-station, the leather chair came from home, and I bought the other one in the antiques market near your place. It was a bit battered, but I found a biggish remnant of rose corded velvet to cover it—a bit faded, but I like that—and there was enough left over for the bed.' Enough, she told herself sharply, and gave him a bright, social smile. 'It's a bit of a surprise to see you here, Lucas, but now you are, do you approve?'

'Very much,' he assured her, and handed her the bag. 'I brought your coat back.'

'Thank you. Come in and close the door. You can put your jacket on the bed.'

Lucas's smile was wry as he removed the jacket to reveal a black roll-neck sweater. 'You know, Emily, when Sedley wouldn't let me in I thought he was acting on your instructions.'

She shook her head and hung the velvet coat in the wardrobe. 'I never expected *you* to come here.'

'I came to grovel, make my peace. Unfortunately, my olive branch got a bit mangled.'

'A soak in some water and the flowers will soon revive,' she said, suddenly feeling breathless. The room seemed to have shrunk in size now they were alone in it together. 'I'll open that wine.'

'Let me do it for you.'

Emily went behind the screen to take a bottle from her tiny fridge and collected glasses and corkscrew from one of her shelves. 'It's not champagne, I'm afraid.'

Lucas removed the cork and poured the wine into the glasses she'd set down on the crowded table. He handed one over and raised his own. 'To your beautiful eyes, Emily Warner,' he said, and tasted the wine.

'To your regained health,' she countered, and drank in turn. 'Do sit down.' She curled up in the smaller chair and Lucas settled himself in the larger one, taking such open pleasure in looking at her that she felt her cheeks grow hot.

'You look very appealing tonight.'

She stared at him in surprise. Her clothes were old and her face was as bare as her feet. The only thing she had going for her was newly washed hair. 'Thank you.'

'I obviously disturbed your work. Is it going well?'

'Surprisingly enough, yes.'

'Why surprising?'

'I've had a lot of distraction lately.'

'To put it mildly. Which brings me to one of the reasons for seeing you.' He gave her a straight black look. 'Emily, I know my choice of phrase was tactless in reference to our mutual problem, but I meant the worst for you, not for me.'

Emily sipped some of her wine, eyeing him over the rim of her glass. 'Very true. I'd be the one left holding the baby.'

His face darkened. 'As I told you, I won't shirk my responsibilities.'

'That's nice.'

'Nice?' He gritted his teeth, then leaned forward, his face urgent. 'If you'll only come to my place when I'm not there, how will you let me know?'

'I'll leave a note on the kitchen jotter.'

He scowled. 'Damnation, Emily, we're not talking groceries here!'

Her chin lifted. 'True. But it's not something I care to discuss over the phone, either.'

Lucas drained his glass. 'You're very calm about this.'

Then she was a fantastic actress. 'Not really.'

He got up to put the glass on the table and looked round at the room. 'If you are pregnant you can't stay here,' he said flatly.

'No,' she agreed. 'Imagine lugging a baby-buggy up those stairs.'

Lucas winced. 'You'll need somewhere else to live.'

Emily got up. 'I'll meet that particular problem—if there is one—when I come to it.'

He looked down at her in silence for a moment. 'I'm going back to work next Monday.'

'Are you fit enough for that?'

'I will be.'

'Then I'll come round to clean that morning, as usual.'

Silence fell between them, and at last Lucas put on

his jacket and took an envelope from the pocket. 'You should have reminded me,' he said huskily.

Emily flushed as she took a cheque from the envelope, her eyes wide when she saw the extravagant amount. Her head flew up. 'What's this for, Lucas? Personal services?'

'Don't talk like that,' he said angrily. 'If you count it by the hour, as we've always done, you'll find it comes out about right. I meant it as a token of appreciation for all you did for me, not an insult.'

Emily badly wanted to tear up the cheque and throw the pieces in his face. Instead she gave it back without drama, her hand steady instead of shaking with fury. 'Make a new cheque out, please. Just give me the usual amount I get every Friday. Or I don't work for you any more.'

Lucas glared at her, a pulse throbbing at the corner of his mouth as he took the cheque, screwed it into a ball, and hurled it into her wastebasket. In angry silence he took his cheque-book out, scrawled his signature and the amount she stipulated, then handed it to her.

'Thank you,' she said politely.

'Are you like this with everyone?' he demanded. 'Or only with me?'

'Like what?'

'In some ways you're the most difficult woman I've ever met.'

'Better than being the easiest,' she retorted, then wished she hadn't when his eyes lit with an unsettling gleam.

Emily swallowed. 'I'm sure you have things to do, so don't let me keep you.'

'You want me to go?'

'Yes.'

'You haven't thanked me for the flowers yet.'

'I'm sure I did.'

Lucas moved closer. 'But not in the way I hoped. I walked all the way here to see you, clutching that damn bouquet, only to get thrown out in the street for my pains, remember. You owe me, Emily Warner.'

'No, I don't.' She backed away, her mouth suddenly dry. 'And I've obviously given you the wrong idea by inviting you to my room.'

He shook his head. 'You made it clear this morning that you don't want me. Which makes no difference. I still want you.'

Too late she realised she had nowhere to go. Lucas had backed her up against the bed, the edge of which fitted nicely behind her knees. If he moved only a fraction, she would fall. She shivered as she pictured all too vividly what might come next.

'Just a kiss, Emily,' he whispered. 'As thanks for the flowers, or goodnight, or whatever reason suits you best—'

At the first touch of his lips on hers Emily's legs buckled. She sat abruptly on the bed and Lucas fell on his knees beside her, hauling her against his chest to kiss her with such force and hunger that she yielded to him, powerless to control her response.

'You see what you reduce me to?' he demanded roughly, raising his head a fraction. 'Does it give you a kick to see me on my knees?'

She shook her head wordlessly, and Lucas stared down into her flushed face for a moment as though expecting her to speak. When she remained silent he released her and got wearily to his feet.

'Time I went, obviously.' He pulled on his jacket and, utterly deflated, Emily scrambled to her feet.

'Thank you for bringing my jacket back.' She took in a deep breath and folded her arms across her chest. 'It's no use. I lied, Lucas. You know very well that I do—' She stopped, biting her lip.

'What?' he demanded, his face tense.

'Want you.'

He lunged towards her in triumph, but she held out fending arms. 'No, Lucas. It doesn't change anything. Even,' she added deliberately, 'if the worst comes to the worst.'

Lucas, abruptly still, gave her a look which raised the hairs on the back of her neck. 'What the hell are you saying? If you are expecting my child, surely you can't expect me to stay tamely out of your life?'

Emily met the look head-on. 'If we had created a child within a relationship it would be different. But in our case it was an accident I keep feeling I should have prevented.'

'How do you work that out? In that particular situation you didn't stand a chance, against me or any other man frantic to make love to you.' Lucas leaned against the door, arms folded. 'Tell me—purely as a hypothesis—if I hadn't been ill, and we'd gone through the accepted mating rituals of dining out and trips to the theatre and so on, before we finally became lovers, would you feel different on the subject?'

'I've no idea, because it doesn't apply in this case. If you hadn't been ill, it wouldn't have happened—any of it,' she said tartly. 'I'm just your cleaner, remember.'

'How could I forget? You keep reminding me often enough.' He looked suddenly tired. 'All right, you win.

But,' he added, his eyes spearing hers, 'keep your promise, Emily.'

'To tell you the worst?' she countered. 'I'll leave a note for you next Monday. I should know by then.'

Lucas gave her a long, hard look, hesitated as though he meant to say something, then, with a muttered curse, opened the door and strode out to race down the stairs at a rate that terrified her. Emily ran to watch him out of sight, but the street door closed so softly it was some time before she went down to make sure he'd gone. And, instead of allowing herself the relief of tears, she looked through Nat's kitchen cupboards to borrow a vase, rescued the undamaged blooms from the sheaf of daffodils and tulips, and carried the result up to her room. Which looked depressingly empty now Lucas had removed his forceful presence from it.

CHAPTER TEN

THE rest of the week dragged by. Emily seized the phone expectantly every time it rang, but it was never Lucas. Not that she had really expected to hear from him after sending him away. But she'd hoped. And missed him so badly by the end of the week that after finishing her Friday session at the Donaldsons' she gave in to impulse and ran across the street to see him. But turned away before she even reached the entrance to his building, afraid Lucas wouldn't even let her through the door.

Emily trudged back to Spitalfields, cleaned Mark's rooms, checked that nothing needed doing in Nat's, went early to bed to toss and turn through another restless night, then woke next morning to find that she was not expecting Lucas Tennent's child after all. Limp with relief, along with other emotions she put down to hormonal imbalance, she rang Lucas immediately, but her euphoria faded when his recorded voice told her to leave a message. Unwilling to entrust this particular piece of news to his answer-machine, Emily was forced to keep to the original, unsatisfactory plan of leaving a note for Lucas after her Monday cleaning session.

Ginny was visiting in-laws with Charlie, so with no Saturday morning rendezvous with her friend to brighten her day, Emily went shopping locally to pass an hour or two. Later, laden with bags, she treated herself to the rare indulgence of a fry-up in the Market Café to put off returning to her room.

From then on, Emily's weekend went rapidly down-

hill. Back in her solitary room, all set to put in a good
few hours on her laptop now her worries were over, she
experienced her first run-in with writer's block. After a
frustrating session of scrapping every sentence the minute it came up on the screen, she gave up at last in
disgust. Feeling headachey and out of sorts, she took her
shopping down to Nat's kitchen and listened to his radio
while she spent a more productive session making vegetable soup and her mother's special recipe for tomato
sauce. Catering sorted for the immediate future, Emily
made sure Nat's kitchen was pristine afterwards, con-
signed her pots of sauce to his freezer, ready for future
pasta suppers, and took her container of healthful soup
up to her room.

Afterwards, Emily stood at the window, staring moodily over the rooftops towards the backdrop of City tow-
ers as she wondered how to fill the rest of the day. One
of the new paperbacks she'd bought or a session in front
of the television were the only options in the ancient,
empty house she'd never actually been alone in before.
Mark was away on a course, Nat was restored to his
wife and family and, worst of all, Lucas's recorded message was the only response to two more phone calls. She
wished now that she'd agreed to go home for the weekend. But when her mother had suggested it Emily had
been waiting for nature to inform her of her fate, too
tense to enjoy a stay in the little cottage her parents had
bought when they vacated the vicarage. But now everything was back to normal again it would have been good
to spend time at home. Andy, his wife Bridget and their
two small sons usually came to share the Sunday roast
when Emily was down, and in her present mood she
would have enjoyed their boisterous company. Instead,
she was rapidly growing bored with her own.

Emily had never welcomed any morning more thankfully than the one which dawned the following Monday. She set off for her cleaning sessions with a feeling of escape, so glad to quit the elegant green walls of her solitary confinement that she walked briskly, revelling in the noise and bustle of traffic and passers-by. But when she left the Donaldsons' immaculate flat later her mood deteriorated as she crossed the cobbled street to Lucas Tennent's building. It would be strange, now, to work there in his absence. She'd given up trying to ring him over the weekend, which meant a note on his kitchen jotter. On her way up in the lift, Emily wondered whether to try for humorous and light or just to ask him to ring her.

But when Emily unlocked Lucas's door a note was unnecessary. He was in the hall, waiting for her. Without a word, he pulled her into his arms and kissed her surprised, parted lips with a hunger she responded to so fiercely she felt his heart thud against her as he yanked her up on tiptoe against his chest.

'Why are you here?' she panted, when she could.

'I'm waiting for you,' he said raggedly, and began kissing her again until Emily found the strength from somewhere to push him away a little.

'Aren't you well?' she demanded, touching a hand to his forehead.

'Now you're here I've never felt better,' Lucas assured her with a triumphant smile. He seized her by the waist and swung her round in a dizzying circle, then set her on her feet with a look of horrified apology. 'Hell, I'm *sorry*—'

'It doesn't matter. I'm not pregnant,' Emily blurted.

Lucas stood utterly still, the animation draining from

his face. 'When did you know?' he said conversation-ally.

'Saturday morning.'

His eyes glittered. 'Two *days* ago? And it never oc-curred to you to contact me?'

Emily's chin lifted. 'Of course it did, but you weren't around. I couldn't leave that kind of message on your machine. So I thought I'd just leave a note today, as promised.'

'Would you have preferred that to telling me face to face?' he demanded.

'No. I'm very glad to see you,' she told him. Which was an understatement. 'You haven't told me why you're at home, by the way.'

'I decided to take more time off.'

'You could have rung to tell me.'

'Do you think I'm a fool, Emily? If I had you wouldn't be here now.' His eyes narrowed, putting her antennae on red alert. 'So. There's no outcome to worry about, after all.'

'No.'

'You must be pleased.'

'Of course I am.' She looked away. 'If you'd rung me over the weekend, I could have put you out of your suspense.'

Lucas took her chin in his hand and raised her face to his. 'You made it pretty plain that night that you wanted nothing more to do with me. Did you really ex-pect me to ring you after that?'

'No,' she said gruffly.

Lucas thawed enough to smile a little. 'I've been away. I went down to visit my mother. The night I came to see you I had some crazy idea about asking you to go with me, but that didn't work out.'

Emily could have cried. After the endless, boring weekend she'd just endured it was painful to think she could have been with Lucas. Even if it had meant meeting his mother.

'I hoped you'd ring, because I wanted to explain things a bit better than I did last time.' She paused, searching for a way to make him understand.

'Go on,' he prompted.

She looked him in the eye. 'The thing is, Lucas, if I had been pregnant I couldn't have handled a relationship with you—of any kind—based on obligation.'

Lucas frowned. 'So if the worst had come to the famous worst, how would you have wanted things arranged? It would have been my child as well as yours. Even if you'd refused to have anything to do with me yourself I would have demanded a father's rights. Unless—' He stopped abruptly.

'Unless what?'

'You'd decided not to go through with it.'

Emily swallowed. 'A termination?'

'Yes,' he said tonelessly. 'Though that never occurred to me.'

She shivered. 'It never occurred to me, either. Good daughter of the vicarage that I am.'

'So you are. I'd forgotten that.' He rubbed a hand over his chin, eyeing her soberly. 'It would have made life doubly awkward for you if there had been a child.'

'Very true,' she agreed. 'I suppose I would have coped somehow; so would my parents. But I'm grateful it didn't come to that. Though if it had I'm sure you and I could have come to an amicable agreement of some kind. About the baby, I mean.'

'I'm glad you think so,' he said dryly. 'But, since there is no baby, where do we go from here?'

'What do you mean?'

'Oh come *on* Emily,' he said impatiently. 'After what happened the moment you were through my door, can you honestly deny the chemistry between us?'

'No, I can't.'

'Then no more of this nonsense about employer and cleaner.' He smiled evilly. 'Or I'll dispense with your services, Miss Warner.'

Her eyes narrowed. 'Would you really do that?'

'Damn right I would, if it was to my advantage.'

'That's not fair,' she said hotly. 'You know I need the money.'

'All's fair in love, Emily!'

'Love?' she snapped. 'Don't you mean lust?'

'I know exactly what I mean,' he cut back.

They stared at each other in hostile silence for a moment, then Lucas held out his hand. 'Come and sit down for a moment.'

'I need to make a start—' she began, then thought better of it. If he really was giving her the sack she wasn't working for free. 'On the other hand, Mr Tennent, if you are dispensing with my services I might as well get back to the jobs I'm paid for.'

Lucas grabbed her hand and pulled her along with him until they reached the familiar sofa.

'Sit,' he commanded.

Emily's eyes flashed fire, but in the end she perched on the very edge of the sofa, her back ramrod-straight.

'Good,' approved Lucas. 'Now listen.'

'If you really want to put an end to my cleaner/employer objections you can stop ordering me about, for a start,' she snapped, and he grinned and sat down beside her.

'That's my girl. Or do you object to the term ''girl''?'

She sniffed. 'It's better than your usual "woman".'

'I like the sound of that,' said Lucas, his eyes softening.

'Well, I don't—'

'I meant "usual". It implies continuity.' He took her hand. 'So let's sort this out. I am thirty-one, single, solvent, and with no significant female presence in my life at this moment in time other than you, Miss Warner. You are—how old?'

'Twenty-four, but—'

'Don't interrupt. You have recently severed all connection with the unspeakable Mr Denny, and unless you met someone new last week I take it there's no man in your life right now other than me.' Lucas leaned close. 'You've seen me at my worst—so no nasty surprises there—we both enjoy each other's company, and physically we're very definitely compatible. Are you with me?'

Emily eyed him narrowly. 'I'm not sure.'

He sighed impatiently. 'Short of handing you my curriculum vitae, Miss Warner, what other information do you need to convince you?'

'Of what, exactly?'

'God, grant me patience! Pay attention—'

'Woman?' she said sweetly.

Lucas disarmed her with a snort of laughter. 'How about "darling", then?'

'In preference to "woman", certainly. And I am paying attention. Do go on.'

'Thank you so much.' He rolled his eyes. 'I'm doing my damnedest to get you to admit that there's no reason why we shouldn't spend time together. Socially. No obligation involved, since you're so hung up on that. So do you?'

'Do I what?'

'Admit it?'

'I suppose so.' She eyed him uncertainly. 'Look, are you dispensing with my services, or not? I've lost the thread somewhere.'

He gave a growl of frustration. 'Back to the money again. Is that all you can think about?'

'Lack of it tends to focus the mind,' she said tartly. 'So have I got the sack?'

Lucas gave her a considering look. 'It all depends.'

'On what?'

'Whether you can work for me, and take my weekly cheque, and at the same time accept me as the man in your life.'

Emily gazed at him in silence, her heart beating thickly. 'I—I'm not sure, Lucas.'

His face darkened. 'About me?'

Emily shook her head, suddenly tired of pretending. 'I meant that if we do see each other socially it seems all wrong to take your money at the same time.'

His response to that was to pull her on to his lap and kiss her until her head reeled. At last, Lucas tore his mouth away and groaned, putting her away from him.

'What's the matter?' said Emily breathlessly.

He smoothed her tumbled curls, smiling ruefully. 'You know damn well—I want to take you to bed.'

She smiled at him challengingly. 'You could burn off surplus energy by helping me clean the flat instead.'

He shook his head. 'Not a chance. I've been away, so the place is still perfect from your labours last week. And you don't have to change the bed,' he added. 'I've already done that.'

'Have you, now?'

He leered at her. 'Your suspicions are perfectly correct, Miss Warner. I had every intention of carrying you off to it the moment you came through the door, and keeping you there for the foreseeable future.'

She grinned. 'Bad luck.'

Lucas bent to kiss her dimple, then went on to plant kisses all over her face, but stopped abruptly when he found tears on her lashes. 'Darling, what's wrong?'

'Nothing at all, now,' she said, sniffing. 'But I've had such a depressing week, Lucas. Ever since you left me, in fact. And this weekend I was alone in the house. Mark was on a course, Nat was with Thea, and Ginny was away with Charlie. So, as if Saturday wasn't miserable enough already, I didn't meet her for coffee as usual, either—' She stopped, her face suddenly hot.

'Miserable?' he asked sharply, his arms tightening around her. 'Why?'

'Hormones,' she muttered, ducking her head, but a relentless hand brought her face up.

'Tell me the truth,' Lucas ordered. 'Were you by any chance miserable because you *weren't* pregnant?'

'Of course not,' she said scornfully. Though she had been. For a split-second.

Lucas kissed the tip of her nose. 'Must you really go back to Spitalfields today?'

'Yes. I still have to earn my living. But I'll come back later.'

'And stay!' He kissed her by way of emphasis.

'You mean spend the nights here, too?' she said huskily, when he raised his head.

Lucas nodded, his eyes glinting. 'And I don't mean in the spare bed. It's always best,' he added virtuously, 'to make things clear from the start. I'd hate you to misunderstand my intentions.'

'Which are?' she demanded.

'Exactly what you think they are,' he said promptly, and gave her a smacking kiss totally different from before. 'It doesn't matter that I can't make love to you right now. I can wait. Somehow. But, just in case you've forgotten, I've recently been ill. I need you here with me, day and night, to complete my cure. I haven't been sleeping well lately.'

'Neither have I.'

'Why?'

'You know perfectly well why,' she said crossly, and tried to get up, but Lucas kept her firmly in place on his lap.

'So why the hell did you send me packing that night?' he demanded.

'Lucas,' she said patiently, 'at that point I could have been pregnant.'

He gave her a baffled glare. 'What's that got to do with it?'

'Everything.' Emily smiled at him coaxingly. 'Surely you can see my point?'

'No,' he said flatly, and ran the tip of his tongue round the outline of her parted lips before sliding it into her mouth, the kiss so arousing it won him a feverish response. But after a breathless, increasingly frustrating interval Emily pushed his hands firmly away.

'Stop! I can't think when you do that, and I need to get a few things straight, Lucas. I'm happy to come back later. Very happy,' she added with a smile. 'The rest of the week, too, if you want, in the time left over from my cleaning jobs. But I'm not going to sleep here.'

He stared incredulously. 'Why the hell not?'

'If I stay here at night it would be the next best thing to moving in with you.'

'What's wrong with that?' he said, and cupped her face in his hands.

'Try to understand, Lucas. My father tries desperately hard to be liberal, but it really upset him when I set up house with Miles. Dad would have liked to see me married first.'

'Which would have been a total disaster!'

Emily nodded vehemently in agreement. 'Dad knows that now, and is probably thanking God daily that there wasn't a wedding. My mother lives in the real world, so her objection was to Miles, not the cohabiting. But the thing is, Lucas,' she went on, 'I'm not going to upset their apple cart again right now by even appearing to move in with you.'

His eyes narrowed. 'You mean you'd hold out for a ring first?'

'Of course not,' she said scornfully. 'I simply want to give them—and myself—time to get over the last fiasco before trying anything like it again.'

'It wouldn't be a fiasco with me,' Lucas said flatly. 'So what exactly *do* you want, Emily?'

'To carry on with my life as usual, spend as much time as you like with you, but go back to Spitalfields at night,' she said, smiling.

'Stop coercing me with that dimple,' growled Lucas. 'What about your novel?'

'I'll take time off from that until you go back to work.'

He smiled indulgently. 'You realise that it won't make the slightest difference?'

'What do you mean?'

The black eyes gleamed with a look so explicit she caught her breath. 'To the precise nature of our relationship, Miss Warner. Go back to your room at night if you must, but no one will be fooled. Sedley knows already.'

'Knows what?'

'How I feel about you.'

'That's nice, because *I* don't!'

'Of course you do. I want you so much I can't sleep at night, Miss Warner.' And to prove his point Lucas kissed and caressed her to a pitch of longing that made it clear that making love would happen any time, or anywhere, the mutual need arose. 'You see?' he said hoarsely, raising his head. 'Everyone will assume we're lovers whether you stay here at night or not.'

'I know that!' said Emily scornfully. 'I'm not an idiot. But I'm sticking to my guns. Indulge me in this, please, Lucas. Or—'

'Or you won't even spend the rest of the morning with me,' he said, resigned.

'I have to get back right now, anyway,' she said, startling him enough to let her go when she jumped to her feet.

'*Why?*'

'Because I have my other jobs to do. After which I need a shower and a change of clothes.'

'In future keep clothes here. Though, personally,' he said, eyeing her, 'I find the dishevelled look *very* sexy. You look perfect to me.'

Because she knew her face was shiny, her hair had escaped from its moorings, and she was wearing jeans so old they were bleached nearly white, Emily eyed him with scorn.

'I mean it,' he assured her, then scowled. 'All right, have it your way. But no walking back. I'll call a cab.' He kissed her swiftly. 'Then, when you're ready, I'll come and collect you.'

'No, don't do that,' she said urgently. 'I'll come back on my own.'

His eyes narrowed. 'Why don't you want me to fetch you?'

Emily braced herself. 'You won't like it.'

'Tell me, anyway.'

'Miles came to fetch me in a taxi when I moved in with him. It was a weekend and there were people around from the other flats. We were waved off like newly-weds.' She eyed him warily. 'Mark will be back from his course this morning, with his girlfriend—'

'So what?' snapped Lucas. 'Do you think they'll care a toss that I'm taking you off with me?'

'*No!* I just don't want it to be like last time. I want everything different. Silly, I know, but I'm superstitious. Try to see it my way.'

'Chauvinist that I am,' he said with cold sarcasm, 'I can only see it from my own. You quite fancy an hour or two here with me now and then, as long as you can sneak away when your friends aren't looking. And I'm supposed to be grateful for that?'

'You're putting words in my mouth,' she said angrily.

'I prefer them to yours!' he snapped, his eyes so hostile she backed away. 'If we are to share our life in any way at all, I want exclusive rights on the arrangement— while it lasts—and I want it public, *darling.*'

The snarled, flippant endearment was the last straw. Emily gave him a look that should have felled him on the spot, then ran for her coat, snatched up her bag, and raced from the flat, banging the door behind her. In the lift angry tears streamed down her face, partly because there'd been no need to run. Lucas had made no attempt to come after her.

*   *   *

When the cab dropped a deeply miserable Emily in Spitalfields she forced a smile when she found Bryony on her way out. 'Morning, Nurse Talbot.'

'Hi, Emily.' Bryony beamed. 'I'm just popping out for a paper.'

'Enjoy your weekend?'

'You bet I did. I made full use of the hotel gym and spa facilities in the day while Mark worked his socks off, then we got together afterwards for the socialising. I didn't trust the females on the course!' Bryony winked as she went to the door, then turned. 'Oh, by the way, I let your brother in just now. He's waiting for you in your room.'

Emily blenched. '*Andy?* Oh, my God, something's wrong at home!' She took the stairs at a run, raced up the second flight, and shot through the open doorway to find a man stuffing her laptop into a sports bag.

'*Miles?* Put that down,' she shouted furiously.

'Emily!' Miles Denny spun round to face her, his dismay quickly covered by belligerence. 'I'm only taking what's mine.'

'Wrong. You're stealing,' she snapped. 'How did you find out where I lived?'

He smiled smugly. 'Ginny keeps an address-book by her telephone.'

'Snooping,' said Emily with disdain. 'But right now you're trespassing. I should call the police.'

He glared at her. 'If you'd returned my calls it needn't have come to this. I just want the laptop.'

'Well, you can't have it. It's mine. I paid for it, remember. I need it.'

'Hard luck,' he sneered. 'So do I.' He strode towards her, but Emily stood her ground.

'Put that down,' she ordered angrily.

'No chance!' He tried to brush her aside, but Emily fought with him, trying to wrench the bag from him, and after a panting, undignified struggle Miles shoved her away roughly at last, sending her sprawling on the bed. But by the time he was through the open doorway with his prize Emily was up and running. She flew across the landing, careering down to wrench the bag away so violently when she caught up with him on the second flight that she missed her footing, and with a scream crashed into Miles. He gave a despairing yell as he tried desperately to save himself, then went hurtling the rest of the way, to land with a sickening crack as his head met the beautiful tiles of the hall floor. The noise brought Mark bursting from his rooms to race down the stairs with a groan of horror when he saw Emily in a winded, crumpled heap, the sports bag clutched to her chest. He crouched to take it from her, his face so white Emily managed a wobbly smile. He heaved a great sigh of relief.

'Thank God! Are you all right? What the hell happened, Em? Who's the guy? Where do you hurt?'

'All—over. Is—is he dead?' she gasped, shivering.

At which point Bryony arrived back, took in the scene, and immediately switched to staff nurse mode. When a groan from the man on the floor indicated he was alive, she checked his vital signs, then gave Emily a thorough going over, her fingers gentle through the tumbled black curls as she encouraged deep breaths. 'I'll see to your brother in a minute. Did you bump your head?'

'No more—than—various other bits of me,' gasped Emily. 'My ankle—hurts most. I stuck my leg out to save myself.'

Bryony tried the patient's endurance not a little with

some expert probing. 'Not broken, but a bad sprain by the look of it. Best to have an X-ray to make sure—you may be concussed, too. We'll take you into hospital, love.'

'What about your brother?' said Mark.

Emily eyed the recumbent, groaning man with scorn only slightly tempered with remorse. 'That's not my brother. He was making off with my laptop—'

'*What?*' screeched Bryony. 'You mean I let a burglar up to your room?'

'Ex-boyfriend, not burglar. How is he?'

Bryony checked Miles's pulse again, then shrugged. 'He's concussed, but as far as I can tell he hasn't broken anything. Not even his neck.'

'Thank heavens for that. I'd hate to have his murder on my conscience. I didn't *mean* to push him down the stairs.' Emily smiled ruefully at Mark. 'Break it to me gently. Is the laptop done for?'

He retrieved the bag, took the machine out and opened it up. 'I can't be sure without switching it on,' he said, examining it. 'I'll check it later.'

Bryony returned her attention to the groaning man on the floor. 'What's his name, Em?'

'Miles Denny.'

'Right then, Miles Denny. Let's have a proper look at you.'

Miles surfaced groggily, ignored Bryony's orders to lie still, struggled upright, threw up copiously and passed out again.

'Yikes!' said Mark in disgust.

During the hectic few minutes that followed Bryony displayed sterling qualities of organisation. She rang for an ambulance, put a bag of ice on Emily's ankle, and with Mark's reluctant, green-faced help cleared up the mess and mopped up the patient while they waited. The paramedics who arrived knew Bryony from her job on the staff at the A & E Department at Guy's Hospital, and much joshing went on about busman's holidays while she gave them concise details of the fall. The unhappy Miles, fully conscious and complaining now, was soon strapped, complete with neck brace, to a stretcher and stowed in the ambulance. Bryony helped Emily inside after him, then jumped in herself for the familiar ride to the hospital.

'I'll do my best to get you seen quickly, Em,' she promised, and cast a worried glance at her as they set off. 'How do you feel?'

Emily gave her a wan little smile. 'Not great. But probably a whole lot better than Miles over there.'

'Nice fellow!' whispered Bryony in her ear. 'When I went up to your room for your bag I found he'd forced the lock and damaged the door while he was at it.'

Emily groaned in dismay. 'Nat won't be happy.'

'I doubt he'll worry over a few splinters.'

'Genuine Georgian splinters, circa 1727!'

Bryony grinned. 'Nat won't care a toss about that, now he's back with Thea and the twins.'

There was an urgent sound from the man opposite, and one of the paramedics caught Emily's eye. 'He wants to talk to you. But you keep that foot where it is, love. He'll have to shout across.'

'What is it, Miles?' asked Emily, craning her neck to see him.

'I'm sorry,' he gasped. 'Is the laptop smashed?'

Bryony glared at him. 'Of course it is. But *just* in case you're interested, Emily sprained her ankle.'

'Buy—her—new computer.' He managed a smile, then passed out again.

It was an hour later before Emily, X-rayed, strapped up and provided with a crutch, finally hobbled from the hospital with Bryony, who had made some enquiries in the meantime, at Emily's urgent request, and learned that Miles was concussed enough to be kept in overnight for observation, but there was no skull fracture.

'Ouch. I didn't think of anything as serious as that.' Emily pulled a face, then smiled warmly at Bryony in the taxi. 'I'm so lucky you were there this morning. You're a star.'

'Nah! As they say on television—just doing my job.'

When they turned down the familiar cobbled street Bryony told the taxi-driver to wait outside the house, and fetched Mark to help Emily from the cab.

'We'd better commandeer Nat's kitchen for the moment,' said Mark when they were inside.

'I'll make tea,' said Bryony, hovering as Emily made slow progress along the narrow hall.

'I need something stronger than tea!' protested Mark, and shuddered. 'It took years off my life when I saw you lying in a heap, Emily. My heart only kicked in again when you smiled at me.'

'Sorry about that.' She grinned at him, glad to sit down at the table.

But it was only after reviving hot tea, when the shock of the past couple of hours began to recede, that the full implications of the episode finally dawned on Emily.

'You know you can't go back to your room like that, Em,' said Mark, looking worried. 'I'd change places like a shot, but you'd still have to get up a flight of stairs to mine.'

'I'll have to go home, I suppose,' said Emily, shrugging.

'Easier stairs there?' asked Bryony, refilling her cup.

'Worse than here, if anything.' Emily thought with misgiving of the steep, open-tread staircase in her parents' cottage. 'I suppose I could beg a bed in my brother's bungalow for a night or two.' But, much as she loved her boisterous nephews, at the moment Emily felt desperate for peace and quiet. 'I don't see what else I can do. I'll ring Andy when he gets home.'

'You need a rest,' said Bryony, and exchanged a look with Mark. 'I think we should put her in Nat's bed for a bit.'

Her voluble protests brushed aside by the other two, Emily eventually gave in, on condition that Bryony helped her into Nat's bathroom first. 'I meant to shower the minute I arrived back, but Miles got in the way. Sorry to be a nuisance, but could you fetch me a change of clothes, too, please?'

'Of course. Tell me what you want and I'll pack a bag for you while I'm at it.'

By the time the shower was over, her hair was reasonably dry, and she was finally propped up under the quilt on Nat's bed, Emily was so limp with reaction she didn't care whose bed it was. 'I'm fine now,' she told her willing helpers. 'Take off and have some time to yourselves.'

Bryony suggested Mark run up to Emily's room for the book she was reading, and he hurried back to report that there was a message on her machine. 'Thought I'd better listen in.'

'Who was it?'

'Some bloke ordering you to ring him. Deep voice, no name.' Mark grinned and handed her his cellphone. 'Use this.'

Emily held the phone in her hand for a long time once she was alone, not sure that talking to Lucas was a good idea. He was probably still angry. And she hadn't changed her mind. She was determined to keep their relationship private so no one would know, this time, when it was over.

Emily keyed in Lucas's number, listened, resigned, to his recorded message, then gave a brief account of the fall that made it impossible to work for him for a while. She hesitated, said a forlorn goodbye and disconnected. At which point her body insisted on rest and she drifted into sleep.

She was jerked awake by an accusing voice and surfaced, dazed, to meet a pair of furious dark eyes glaring at her from a small, all-too-familiar face.

'What are you doing in my husband's bed?' demanded Thea Sedley.

CHAPTER ELEVEN

EMILY sat up, speechless with horrified dismay, which she saw reflected in Nat's eyes as he peered over his wife's shoulder. But before she could gather her wits to explain Bryony and Mark came hurtling downstairs to save her the trouble. Halfway through their story Nat went out to answer a peremptory rapping on the front door, and Lucas Tennent came into the bedroom like a whirlwind, brushed everyone aside and took Emily into his arms.

She clung to him convulsively, burying her face against his sweater, so giddy with relief she wanted to howl like a baby now there was nothing to cry about. 'Miles broke into my room, Lucas. He wanted the laptop—'

'To hell with the laptop!' Ignoring the fascinated on-lookers, he turned her face up to his to kiss her, his mouth tightening when he saw the bruise on her cheek. 'In your message you said the bastard's in hospital. Pity—I'd like a word with him.'

Emily chuckled, her wet eyes suddenly dancing. 'No need to beat Miles up, Lucas. He didn't cause the bruises; I sort of bounced off him against the wall. I was the one who damaged *him*—and without a cricket bat this time, too.'

'God, you're a dangerous woman!' He kissed her again, then stood up. 'I'm taking you home.'

Home. Emily smiled up at him, liking the sound of that. 'OK. But first let me make some introductions. You know Nat, but this is his wife, Thea. And this is Bryony Talbot and Mark Cooper, my saviours.'

Lucas shook hands all round while Emily described how Bryony and Mark had come to her rescue.

'Bryony did all the work,' said Mark proudly.

'What a fright you've had!' To Emily's surprise, Thea came up to the bed and kissed her cheek. 'Sorry I yelled. Appearances were deceptive.' She smiled at Lucas. 'Nat said you were tall, dark and handsome.'

Lucas flushed, to Emily's deep enjoyment, gave Thea a mocking little bow, then thanked Bryony and Mark for their help. 'I can take over now.'

'You said you were taking her home, but where do you live?' asked Bryony bluntly. 'She can't use that foot for a while.'

'It's a top-floor apartment overlooking the river, with a nice comfortable lift instead of death-defying stairs. No offence,' Lucas told Nat with a grin.

'None taken.' Nat gave Emily a rueful smile. 'So all the precautions were in vain. Your ex-swain managed to get in after all.'

'He just rang the bell to ask for Emily, and I let him in,' said Bryony with remorse. 'He told me he was her brother, the wretch.'

'Talking of Andy,' said Nat, 'does your family know about this, Emily?'

She shook her head. 'I was going to ring Andy when he gets home from school, and ask for board and lodging for a bit—'

'You don't need that now,' cut in Lucas. 'You can ring your mother from the flat.'

'Where did you two meet?' asked Thea curiously.

Emily exchanged a gleaming look with Lucas. 'Like Nat, he employs me. I'm his cleaner.'

He shook his head. 'Not any more. Your cleaning days are over.'

'Only until my foot gets better!'

'We'll discuss it later,' he said firmly, and held out his arms. 'Up you come.'

'I can walk with the aid of my trusty crutch,' she protested, but Lucas shook his head.

'At the moment, I feel this overwhelming compulsion to hold you in my arms,' he said, not quite lightly, and won looks of warm approval from Thea and Bryony. 'Besides, you look a bit fragile.'

'So would you in my place,' she said, grimacing. 'Though it was Miles who fell down and broke his crown.'

'Good,' said Lucas with grim satisfaction. 'But did he really come here just to make off with the laptop?'

'Apparently.'

'Maybe he's left something on the hard drive,' suggested Mark. 'I checked it, and it seems to be working. You can play with it later to make sure, Em. I've put it with your bags in the hall.'

Nat went out to answer the door, then returned to say the taxi-driver wanted to know how much longer he had to wait. 'I told him you were ready to go, Lucas. Take good care of her,' he added.

'Don't worry; I will,' Lucas assured him.

Bryony helped Emily to her feet. 'All right, Em?'

'Thanks to you, Nurse, yes.'

'OK, Lucas; she's all yours.'

'That she is.' Lucas picked Emily up, went the round of the others so they could kiss her goodbye, then carried her outside to the taxi waiting on double yellow lines outside in the cobbled street. Nat handed in the crutch and bags, then stood with the others to wave them off, giving Emily a sense of *déjà vu*. So much for keeping Lucas a secret. Barring a different cast of extras, the scene was identical to last time with Miles.

Lucas eyed her face, reading her mind with accuracy. 'Your plan to keep me a secret backfired big time.'

'I don't care. I'm just grateful you arrived when you did.' She giggled. 'Thea had just discovered me in Nat's bed when you came charging in like the cavalry.'

He shook with laughter. 'Not your day, one way and another. Never mind,' he consoled her, taking her hand. 'I promise to make it better from now on. How do you feel after all your adventures, darling? Shall I put you straight to bed when we get home?'

'Good heavens, no!' Emily smiled at him cheerfully. 'Your sofa will do very nicely, thank you. In fact,' she added, 'I could even perch on one of the stools in the kitchen and supervise supper, if you like.'

'Unnecessary.' He gave her a smug look. 'When you left I was furious—'

'I noticed.'

'Don't interrupt. So I went for a walk to cool off while I planned my next course of action, which was to storm over to Spitalfields and carry you off over my shoulder if necessary. Being the practical type, I did some shopping on the way back to the flat so I could feed you after the kidnapping.' His jaw clenched. 'Imagine my reaction when I heard your message.'

'Thank you for coming to my rescue, Lucas.' Emily stretched a little, wincing when her ankle protested.

'I wanted to collect you in my new car,' he said with regret, 'but I knew there'd be nowhere to park near Nat's house, so I fell back on a cab.'

'What kind of car?'

'A new model Mini Cooper S,' he said, trying to sound offhand.

'Really?' Emily smiled, surprised. 'I would have thought something like a Porsche was more in your line.'

'Why?'

'It goes with the rest of you—the hip loft apartment, the job, and so on.'

'I do own something speedier for motorway journeys, also bought from new.' His face set. 'In my teens I had to wear blazers and shirts from the school second-hand shop. So these days I like my possessions brand-new.'

Emily was quiet for the rest of the short journey, and Lucas, his eyes concerned, put his arm round her and held her protectively. When they arrived at his building Emily would have given much to get inside under her own steam, but common sense told her that walking with a crutch would be a precarious business on a cobbled street. And there was no point in risking another injury. She'd had quite enough excitement for one day.

The helpful taxi driver parked as near to the entrance as possible, then brought the bags inside and put them in the lift while Lucas carried Emily in to set her down very carefully, holding her by the waist.

'Lean against me while I pay up. Keep the weight off your foot.'

Emily did as she was told, shivering a little despite the warmth of the lift.

'You're cold,' he said, hugging her close as the lift doors closed on the lavishly-tipped driver.

'Probably reaction. Bryony warned me about that.'

'Quite a girl, isn't she? Your friend Mark's a lucky man. Up you come,' he added as the lift doors opened. 'I'll soon have you safe and sound on our sofa.'

Emily felt a little warmer at the discovery that Lucas

shared her views about his sofa. Which, of course, didn't mean she was the only woman who'd ever sat there with him.

'That's a strange look on your face,' commented Lucas, as he carried her into the hall. He was breathing heavily by the time they reached the big, split-level living-room she loved so much. He lowered her carefully to the sofa, stacked cushions behind her, bent to give her a swift kiss, then straightened to heave in a deep breath. 'I'm out of condition. Now stay put,' he ordered. 'I'll get the bags in from the hall. Don't move a muscle until I get back.'

Emily had no desire to move any muscles, particularly those in the ankle stretched out in front of her on the sofa. She lay motionless, glad to be so comfortable after all the hassle, her only mobile feature her eyes as she looked around her at the uncluttered space of Lucas's living-room. The great advantage of any loft apartment was light. Lucas's was filled with it, even on a rainy day. And now she was going to live here. At least for a while.

'You look very thoughtful,' said Lucas, rejoining her. 'Ankle hurting?'

'Not much, now. But I must give Mother the news before she hears it from Thea.'

'Will she expect you to go home to recuperate?' he asked, frowning.

'In theory, yes. But their new cottage is actually very old, with open-tread stairs as steep as Nat's.'

'In that case, you're much better here with me. Ask your parents to visit you here instead. Your friend Ginny, too.' His lips twitched as he bent to pat her cheek. 'Don't look so stunned. It won't commit you to anything.'

'That's very kind of you,' said Emily, ignoring the last bit, 'but for the time being I'll just tell Mother I've hurt my ankle. She's never seen Nat's stairs.'

Lucas handed her his cellphone. 'Give her the number and tell her to ring you on that. Tell her you've borrowed it until the ankle's better.'

She smiled at him gratefully and reached for the crutch.

'What's the matter?' he demanded.

'I'm going to the bathroom, *and* I'm going to manage on my own with this,' she said firmly. 'You'll put your back out if you keep carrying me everywhere.'

'But I like the feel of you helpless in my arms!'

Emily made a face at him, and carefully got to her feet. Bryony had advised against trousers with a strapped ankle and, to make life easier, had eased Emily into a skirt and tunic in ribbed topaz wool, normally kept for special occasions. Because the skirt was long, the outfit called for boots or high heels, but with a single flat black loafer on her good foot Emily felt more like Long John Silver than Cinderella. She tucked the crutch under her arm and, with Lucas pacing beside her, flatly refusing to let her go it alone, she made with increasing agility for the bathroom, then closed the door in his face. Afterwards, Emily opened it to find him standing where she'd left him.

'We're back to the unromantic intimacy again,' she said, resigned.

'Works for me!' Lucas picked her up, ignoring her protests. 'Stop arguing, Emily. It's a waste of time.' He gave her a questioning look as he set her down on the sofa again. 'I've been thinking of what Mrs Sedley said to you. Is that really how you see me?'

She looked blank for a moment, then her eyes lit with

unholy glee. 'Oh, tall, dark and handsome, you mean? That's Nat's description, not mine.'

Lucas looked so appalled she roared with laughter, and reassured him that it was Nat's way of diverting his wife's suspicions from his lady lodger. 'He said it was the first thing that came into his head when Thea asked. Which was before he met you, anyway,' added Emily, and batted her eyelashes. 'But if the cap fits…'

To her surprise, colour rose in the lean, watchful face. 'Do *you* think it fits?' he asked casually.

'Like a glove, Mr Tennent. You're the archetypal answer to a maiden's prayer—' She halted abruptly, and he frowned and took her hand.

'What's the matter? Are you in pain?'

'No.' She gave him an unhappy look. 'I keep thinking of something you said. About a school uniform from the second-hand shop.'

Lucas looked blank for a moment, then gently slid his arms round her as comprehension dawned. 'Surely you're not saying that *you* feel second-hand after Miles?'

'I didn't until I met you,' she said honestly, pleased that he understood. 'I'd had boyfriends before, relationships that ran their course and ended amicably. But after Miles I felt so grubby and humiliated.' She met his eyes squarely. 'And you do seem rather fixated on the new and unsullied.'

'Only when it comes to cars and clothes!' Lucas gave her a swift, punitive kiss. 'Though, oddly enough, what I feel for you *is* new. I've known quite a few women, obviously. It would be pretty strange if I hadn't at my age—'

'And with your various impressive assets,' she put in slyly.

'As I was saying,' he said with severity. 'I've known

women in the past, and enjoyed their company both in and out of bed, with no strings and no harm done on either side. But you're different, Emily.'

'Why?'

His eyes locked with hers. 'Because I'm in love with you, of course. And because I can't think of another soul, barring Alice and my mother, who would have cared for me when I was ill. Admittedly, I've never *been* ill before—'

'I could tell!' said Emily, flippant to hide the great bubble of joy rising inside her.

'Because I made such a fuss?'

'Exactly.'

'But you still hung in there and got me through it. And in return I was idiot enough to risk getting you pregnant,' he added bitterly.

'I didn't think about risks at the time—or anything else,' Emily assured him. 'Making love with you put my thought processes out of action. I'd never experienced anything like that before. Especially the last bit.' Her eyes locked with his. 'Was that a fluke, do you think? Or will it happen next time, as well?'

Lucas let out a shout of laughter. 'Are you by any chance propositioning me, Miss Warner?'

'Purely in the interest of scientific experiment,' she said primly, then dimpled at him in a way which brought an abrupt end to the conversation.

'This won't do,' said Lucas, after an interval of kisses and caresses which quickly threatened to get out of hand. 'I said you were a dangerous woman. You're driving me insane.'

'Me, too,' she said with feeling, then blushed as her stomach gave a loud, unromantic rumble.

'Darling, you're hungry—and I haven't even given

you a cup of tea!' He jumped up in remorse. 'I'll make up for it right now. Just sit there while I do something about feeding you.'

'I'm coming, too,' she insisted, reaching for the crutch.

'Why?' he said, exasperated.

'I just want to be where you are,' she said simply.

Lucas scooped her up, holding her high against his chest as he kissed her in a way which made words superfluous. 'My sentiments exactly,' he said huskily at last, then carried her off to deposit her on one of his smart retro stools. 'Now, just sit there and watch while I switch on the oven.'

Lucas's idea of playing chef was to put together plates of cold, herb-stuffed chicken and Bayonne ham, served with salad greens and several kinds of cheese. The sole function of the oven, Emily discovered, laughing, was to heat a baton of French bread to accompany the meal.

'This is lovely,' she said indistinctly, when they were back on the sofa together.

'The food, or being with me?' asked Lucas, buttering bread for her.

'Both. I spent last weekend almost entirely alone, with my own home-made vegetable soup for every meal.' She made a face. 'I shan't want any more of that for a while.'

'I told my mother about you,' he said casually, startling her. 'Described how you came to nurse me in my hour of need.'

Emily put her fork down, her eyes wide. 'She must have been taken aback—that your cleaner came to the rescue, I mean?'

Lucas wagged an admonishing knife. 'I told her that your cleaning jobs finance you while you're writing a novel. She was impressed, and wants to meet you. When you're mobile again I'll drive you down for Sunday lunch.'

Emily gazed at him in silence.

'As I keep saying, it won't commit you to anything,' he assured her.

'You take a lot of women to meet your mother?'

'No. You'll be the first.'

The information gave Emily a rosy glow which lasted right through supper, though she firmly resisted when Lucas coaxed her to talk about her novel.

'You can read it when I've finished it,' she conceded eventually. 'But only when I'm satisfied with it myself. If I ever am.'

'If you're not, will you give up cleaning and go back to the work you were doing before?'

Emily shook her head. 'I don't want to do that any more. It pays well, and I'm pretty good at it. But I've been far happier with the way my life is now than I ever was at nine-to-fiving in an office. So, if the first novel doesn't turn out well, I'll just try again. I'm sure I can find an extra cleaning job to pay my way.'

'I've thought of something else you can do,' said Lucas casually.

'Really? What, exactly?'

'I'll get rid of this stuff, make some coffee, then I'll explain.' He smiled at her as he hefted the loaded tray. 'Be good while I'm gone.'

CHAPTER TWELVE

WHEN Lucas got back with the coffee, he found Emily with the laptop on her knees. 'I told you to be good,' he said, exasperated. 'Which didn't mean starting work the minute I turned my back.'

She smiled guiltily. 'After I rang my mother I just had to make sure the machine still worked, Lucas. And, as far as I can tell, it does. But I can't help wondering why Miles was so desperate to get it back. I checked when I first took it, of course, but his files were all empty.'

'There must be something lurking on it somewhere.' Lucas sat down beside her. 'Hand it over. I'll do a search.'

'But surely he'd have saved anything important on a disk?'

'I would. But he wasn't expecting you to steal it that night, so there must be something he didn't have time to transfer.'

But other than Emily's novel there was nothing until at last Lucas found a file hidden inside another.

'Bullseye! Our lad has a digital camera.'

Emily, sitting close to look, stiffened in horror when a photograph appeared, filling the entire screen.

Lucas swore volubly and lowered the lid. 'Don't look any more. I'll switch the bloody thing off—'

'No,' said Emily decisively. 'I might as well know the worst. Keep going.'

Three photographs filled the big screen one by one. The studies were of three muscular, nude young men, their smiles provocative as they postured for the photographer. Two of them were strangers to Emily, but the other one delivered sandwiches to the firm she'd once worked for. Where Miles was still employed.

'Get rid of them, please,' she begged.

'Done.' Lucas wiped the laptop clean of everything other than the embryo novel, took it up to his desk on the gallery, then returned to the sofa. He filled cups with strong black coffee and gave one to Emily. 'You need this, darling. You're white as a sheet.'

She drank the hot, fragrant liquid down, reviving as the warmth spread through her. 'How could I have been such a fool?' she said at last. 'Though I wasn't the only one. I was warned about Miles by more than one friend at the firm. His reputation as a womaniser was well-publicised.'

Lucas took her empty cup and put hard, protective arms round her. 'A deliberate smokescreen to keep his proclivities in the closet? Though he isn't the first to feel attracted to both sexes.'

Emily leaned against him gratefully. 'No wonder he would never let me use the laptop. He always kept it in work. But he had it with him when he got in that night, and after the row, when I got violent, he was in such a hurry to take off he left it behind. Poor Tamara,' she added ruefully. 'Miles deliberately let me think he'd been with her that evening.'

'Preferable to the truth.'

'But I could have confronted the girl.'

'He banked on your not believing her if she denied it.'

'You're right.' She leaned her head back to look at Lucas. 'The firm we both worked for is a tad on the conventional side, so he wouldn't want anything getting out to affect his career prospects. It seems my money wasn't my only attraction for Miles. I was his cover, too.'

'And if he's in his right mind again by this time he's probably sweating blood because you still have the blasted laptop,' said Lucas, rubbing his cheek over her hair.

'Actually, he's not,' said Emily with regret. 'In the ambulance Bryony was so angry he hadn't asked about me she told him it was smashed. The smile he gave me must have been relief, not remorse.'

'I could pay him a visit to put him in the picture,' Lucas said grimly.

'Ugh! Don't talk about pictures.'

'If you feel like that, get rid of the blasted machine.'

'Certainly not. I paid good money for it.'

'I'll buy you another one.'

Emily shook her head decisively. 'I can't let you do that.'

'Yes, you can.' He smiled down at her. 'Where's the harm in a present?'

'If you give me cheques *and* buy me presents I'll feel like a kept woman!'

'Hold the thought. Because I am going to keep you.' Lucas stroked her cheek. 'You look tired. You should be in bed.'

'Cuddle me a bit first?'

He drew in a deep breath, his hands sliding beneath the clinging wool tunic as he kissed her. 'Is this what you mean by cuddling?' he demanded against her mouth.

'Whatever it is, I like it,' she whispered, kissing him with such fervour they were soon lying full length together on the sofa, caressing each other into a state of arousal which forced Lucas to pull away at last.

'I'd better take you to bed,' he panted.

She nodded with enthusiasm, licking the tip of her tongue round her swollen lips as she put herself back together.

Lucas clenched his jaw. 'I meant the spare bed!'

'Of course.' She gave him a wicked little smile. 'But I'm afraid you may have to help me undress later, if I get stuck.'

He growled something under his breath. 'Right. Up you come, then.'

'No,' she said firmly. 'I must start fending for myself. I'll call if I need you.'

Lucas jumped up, pushing the hair back from his damp forehead. 'Then for God's sake be careful.'

'Just give me ten minutes. Have a drink, or something.'

'Good idea,' he agreed, his face tense as Emily disdained his aid as she reached for the crutch and got to her feet.

'I'll leave my shoe,' she said, and began a careful progress to the bathroom, leaving Lucas to pour himself a finger of Scotch instead of chasing after her, as he so very obviously wanted to.

Emily hurried through her preparations for the night, removed her clothes, laid them neatly on the chest, slid into bed, and waited.

It seemed a long time before she heard Lucas open the door of the guest room.

'Emily!' he roared. 'Where are you?'

'In here.'

He strode into the master bedroom, then stopped dead when he found her in his bed with the covers drawn up to her chin.

'Ah,' he said, swallowing. 'Of course. I'll take the

other room. Better for you here, with a bathroom close to hand.'

'For heaven's sake, man,' said Emily impatiently. 'Get your kit off and come to bed.'

'Darling,' he said in desperation. 'I can't *do* this. I'm not superhuman—'

'Lucas.' She smiled slowly, bringing her dimple into play. 'In case you're missing the point, I'm doing my darnedest to seduce you!'

He started throwing off his clothes before the words were out of her mouth. He dived into bed and took her into his arms, his breath leaving him in a rush when he found she was naked.

'You undressed yourself,' he accused, sliding a hand over her breasts. 'I was looking forward to giving you a helping hand.'

'I like the one you're giving me now,' she gasped. He laughed deep in his throat and kissed her fiercely, his hands on her bottom to pull her hard against him as her lips opened in welcome and her tongue answered his with caresses of its own.

'I don't want to hurt you—your ankle,' he said hoarsely.

'You won't,' Emily assured him, and felt the muscles of his back tense as her fingers caressed them, digging a little in demand, desire bright and hot inside her as their kisses grew wilder.

'Slowly,' panted Lucas, putting her away a little. 'I was in too much of a rush before. This time I want you to experience every nuance of pleasure possible.'

'You were half-asleep last time,' she said, shivering as his mouth closed over a hard, expectant nipple.

'Not for long.' Lucas raised his head to gaze down

into her glittering eyes. 'And this time I'm very much awake, so pay attention.'

'If you keep the light on,' she said breathlessly, 'you'll see my bruises.'

'And kiss them better.' Lucas drew the covers down until he could see all of her, bruises and all. 'This is part of the deal, darling. I want to see you. I want you to see me. To use all the senses. To touch.' He kissed her mouth as he caressed her breasts. 'Taste.' He took a nipple into his mouth and she moaned, trying to pull him close, but he shook his head, gazing down at her from the tumbled black curls over every part of her body, which grew taut and flushed, her nipples standing proud, as though he were caressing her with his hands, instead of just his glittering, possessive eyes.

'To hear?' she demanded at last, shifting restlessly beneath the tactile gaze.

'God, yes! The sound of that husky little moan sends me crazy,' he said roughly, and kissed her, his lips and tongue taking full possession of hers before his mouth moved down her throat to descend slowly and tantalisingly over her breasts and stomach until he reached the delta between her thighs, and she arched like a strung bow as his tongue played havoc with a part of her unused to such ravishing attention.

Emily lay limp in his arms afterwards, and Lucas held her close, moving a gentling hand down her spine.

'Not a fluke, then,' she said gruffly. 'Or doesn't it count that way?'

'All ways count if they give you pleasure.' He moved over her until he lay propped with his thighs between hers. 'Just to be in total contact like this is a pleasure in itself.'

Her breathing quickened as her eyes locked with his.

'But that,' she whispered, 'is because we know it's just the overture to what comes next.'

She felt him tense in response, his body poised over hers, and slid her hand down between them to caress the part of him which rose, hard and ready in her grasp. 'Now,' she said fiercely, and Lucas obeyed, entering her with a long, slow thrust that pierced her entire body with sensation so intense she gave a sobbing moan. He began to make love to her with a slow-burning control that she responded to with such passionate fervour his control gave way at last to breathless, thrusting frenzy, which brought them to almost simultaneous release and left them gasping in each other's arms as the aftershocks died away.

'I'm getting good at this,' panted Emily, once she regained the power of speech.

Lucas grinned and eased himself on to his back, taking her with him to lie in the crook of his arm. 'It won't work with anyone else,' he warned.

'I know.' Emily heaved a deep, relishing sigh. 'I really thought it was my fault, Lucas.'

He smoothed her damp curls back from her forehead. 'With Miles?'

'Yes. Because it was so—so sort of perfunctory and disappointing.' She looked up at him, smiling ruefully. 'And all the time it was just because I was the wrong gender.'

'Whereas you suit me in every way there is,' said Lucas with emphasis.

'Then that's all that matters.'

'You mean that?'

'Yes.'

'In that case, could we rewind to the point, earlier

today, when I mentioned that I was in love with you, Miss Warner?'

She nodded, flushing. 'I'm in love with you, too, Mr Tennent. Which is a bit frightening.'

'Why?'

'Because we've known each other such a short time.'

'There are no hard and fast rules in relationships, darling.' Lucas bent his head to kiss her. 'Say it again.'

'I love you,' she muttered, ducking her head, but he brought her face up to his.

'I love you, too. So what shall we do about it?'

'I thought we'd just done something quite earth-shattering about it! At least, it was for me.'

Lucas's arm tightened round her. 'For me, too. So much so that I'd hoped to repeat the experience as soon as is humanly possible. But it isn't yet.'

'Isn't what?'

'Possible. You're dynamite, Miss Warner. And, as I said before, I'm not super-human.'

Emily smiled at him. 'You are to me, Mr Tennent.'

'In that case, you're one of a kind, so I'd better hang on to you—' He stopped abruptly. 'Darling, in the heat of the moment I forgot to ask. How's your ankle?'

'Throbbing a bit,' she said, surprised, then grinned. 'But every other part of me was throbbing so much just now I didn't notice.'

Lucas gave a shout of laughter and hugged her close. 'I'd expected to toss and turn all night, thinking of you on the other side of the wall. Instead—' He paused.

'Instead?' Emily prompted.

'We made magic together,' he said softly, a note in his voice which brought her arms round his neck in passionate agreement.

After a while Emily pulled away, a resigned expression on her face. 'And now, alas, I must interrupt this magic moment to request my crutch. Plus my dressing-gown from my bag.'

'Borrow mine,' said Lucas, and slid out of bed to pull on his jeans.

Emily got out of bed, flushing with embarrassment as she tried to balance naked on one foot. Lucas laughed, kissed her, wrapped her in his robe, then scooped her up to deposit her in his bathroom.

'I'll fetch your bags. Shout when you want me.'

Emily put her weight on her good foot to wash her hands afterwards, and eyed her flushed face in the mirror, surprised to find she looked much the same as usual. Her mouth was red, and obviously much kissed, and her eyes were a bit heavy, but they gleamed like the amber earrings she kept for special occasions. Otherwise, the most ravishing experience of her entire life had left no visible mark.

She told Lucas so as he carried her back to bed.

'Did you expect to see a scarlet "A" branded on your forehead?' he said, amused.

'Doesn't apply—we weren't committing adultery.'

'No. We were making love,' he agreed as he slid into bed. 'And I do mean *love*, Miss Warner, not lust. There's a difference.'

'I know.' Emily sighed with pleasure as her body fitted to his as though custom-made for the purpose. They lay together, completely at peace for a comfortable interval, then something occurred to her. 'In all the excitement, I forgot. Earlier you mentioned some other kind of job for me.'

Lucas nodded. 'I did.'

Emily pulled away a little so she could see his face. 'What kind of job? Cleaning at your bank?'

'Hell, no,' he said, appalled.

'What, then?'

Lucas eyed her warily. 'It's not a job exactly.'

'What, then?'

'First,' he said tantalisingly, 'a question or two. When you found you weren't expecting my baby you said you were relieved. Why, exactly?'

She stared at him. 'I would have thought it was obvious.'

'Tell me just the same.'

'For one thing, I really didn't fancy the role of single mother. I couldn't have stayed at Nat's place, and I wouldn't have wanted to go home to my parents. And, quite apart from that, all this would never have been possible.'

'All this?'

'Being here with you, making love with you, having you in my life in any way at all, other than financial support I couldn't have refused. Of course I was relieved. But at the same time, Lucas,' she added, smiling, 'utterly astonished that an experience like that *didn't* result in a baby.'

He let out a deep unsteady breath. 'You certainly know the right things to say to a man, Miss Warner.'

'Actually, I don't. I'm not into flattery.'

'*I* was disappointed,' he said abruptly.

Emily drew away in dismay. 'When we first made love?'

'No! This morning, when you told me you weren't expecting my baby.'

Emily gazed at him in disbelief, her eyes like saucers.

'It's the simple truth,' he assured her, then raised an eyebrow at her change of expression. 'What?' he demanded.

'When I found out, I was disappointed, too—but only for a second or two,' she added honestly. 'But it really amazes me that you were.'

'It amazed me for a while, too. I'd never given fatherhood a thought before.' He smoothed a caressing hand over her stomach. 'Which brings me back to the subject of your future employment. I need a mother for these unborn children of mine. Since you're the only woman in the world I want for the post, Miss Warner, will you accept?'

Emily looked at him in silence for a moment or two, then saw a pulse throbbing at the corner of his mouth and realised that Lucas wasn't sure how she'd respond. 'Yes, please,' she said, her voice even huskier than usual. 'Do you need references?'

Lucas drew in a deep breath. 'No. But before you accept the post there's something you have to do first,' he told her, his voice not quite steady.

'What is it?'

'You have to marry me.'

'*Marry* you?'

Lucas propped himself up on an elbow to look down at her stunned face. 'Emily Warner, you said yes a minute ago.'

'I didn't know what you meant!'

'I've never proposed before, so I obviously didn't get it quite right—' He halted, frowning down at her. 'Wait a minute. You mean you were ready to take me—and these mythical children of mine—without a wedding first?'

'Yes.'

'Even knowing your father's views on the subject?'

Emily gave him a startled look. 'I clean forgot about that. I just wanted to say yes to whatever *you* wanted.'

'My darling girl!' He dived down beside her and took her in his arms. 'So you do love me.'

'I said I did,' she said tartly. 'What else do I have to do to convince you?'

Lucas pretended to consider. 'First you kiss me.'

'That sounds easy.'

'Then you put your arms round me.'

'Like this?'

'Perfect.'

She wriggled closer. 'Now what do I do?'

'Use your imagination,' he said unsteadily.

Emily's imagination proved astoundingly fertile for someone who, up to meeting Lucas Tennent, had considered the entire concept of lovemaking over-rated.

'Are you—convinced yet?' she demanded at one stage, her only answer a devouring kiss as Lucas slid home between her parted thighs and Emily strained him close, her body answering his as she tried to prove to him beyond all doubt how much she loved him. And knew she'd succeeded when he gasped in elation as the earthy, transient glory finally overwhelmed them.

The week that followed was hectic. Emily had grown quite agile with her crutch by the time her parents came to the flat for a celebration lunch everyone much enjoyed after Lucas had formally requested, and been granted, the hand of the Reverend Richard Warner's daughter in marriage. Claire Warner, it was obvious, took to her prospective son-in-law on sight, and to Emily's relief told her in private that her father was equally pleased with her choice.

The next celebration was a party with a guest-list which included a jubilant Ginny Hart, and husband Charlie, along with the Donaldsons, Bryony, Mark, Nat and even Thea, who came up to London for the occasion. And at the weekend Emily, minus crutch, but stiff with nerves, went with Lucas to collect his sister from Heathrow. Alice Tennent, all bronze skin and sun-streaked hair, courtesy of the Italian sun, embraced her brother and Emily with equal enthusiasm, so delighted at the news that she talked wedding plans non-stop with Emily as Lucas drove them down to the house he'd bought for his mother in a Cotswold village near enough to Chastlecombe to invite Emily's family for lunch.

Emily felt rather dazed on the journey back to London that evening.

'Are you tired, sweetheart? Ankle hurting?' asked Lucas.

'No. Neither. I just feel I'm in a dream and I'll wake up any minute. Your mother's lovely, Lucas, and Alice is a kindred spirit, as I'm sure you could tell. I hope they both like me.'

'Of course they do,' he said, laughing. 'And even if they don't it doesn't matter a damn, because I like you. I like you a lot.'

Emily grinned at him. 'I like you a lot, too.' She paused. 'But I'm very glad your mother took to me, just the same.'

'When we had a minute together before we left she told me she was delighted. Relieved, too.'

'Relieved?'

'Because I work in the City, Mother was always afraid I'd marry some frightening, power-suited female in the same line of work.'

'Whereas I've never frightened anyone in my life.'

'I wouldn't say that. You've put the fear of God into Miles Denny more than once!'

'Don't remind me!' Emily shuddered. 'This time I really thought I'd killed him. Thank heavens his skull is thick—but never mind Miles. I'm just glad your mother liked me.'

'She knows that with you I'll have the kind of marriage she never had herself. She wants the same for my sister, too.'

'Does Alice have someone in her life?'

'She's never short of male company, but so far no one significant.' He grinned. 'Ally thinks it's wonderful that I'm marrying my angel of mercy.'

Emily chuckled. 'I'm no angel, Lucas.'

'For which—at certain times—I'm passionately grateful,' he said, in a tone which took her breath away.

By the time Lucas returned to his job in the City, Emily was mobile again, and to please her parents went down to Chastlecombe to spend the month before the wedding with them before taking up permanent residence in Lucas's flat. She spent the weekends with Lucas in London and back home during the week, in the time left over from wedding arrangements, Emily worked on her novel. And found that writer's block was a thing of the past.

'I probably shouldn't be staying here so near to the wedding,' remarked Emily, the Sunday before.

'Why not?' demanded Lucas.

'My superstitions again, I suppose.'

'Because of bloody Miles!'

'I just don't want anything to go wrong this time.'

Lucas moved closer on the sofa and scooped her close against him. 'Nothing,' he assured her, 'will go wrong. I wouldn't dare let it, because Ally will kill me if she can't wear the hat she's bought.'

Emily giggled and relaxed against him. 'It's going to

be a long, long week until Saturday. I'll miss you,' she said, sighing.

'Not as much as I'll miss you,' he said gloomily. 'I'll be so haggard from insomnia you won't recognise me when you come down the aisle.'

'You'll just have to wear a gardenia in your button-hole so I don't marry the wrong man.'

'Fat chance of that.' He laughed and got up, pulling her to her feet. 'Bedtime.'

'It's only a little after ten!'

'I get up early,' he reminded her, then caught her close and kissed her. 'Which, as you know perfectly well, is nothing to do with it.'

It was a wrench to part with Lucas early next morning. Emily clung to him as they said goodbye, as though they were parting forever.

'I'll ring you tonight—and every night,' he said huskily. 'Take care of yourself, please. Don't fall down any more stairs.'

She nodded dumbly, trying to smile, and Lucas kissed her again, then with reluctance broke away. 'See you in church, darling.'

On the way down to Chastlecombe by train later Emily tried hard to dispel the uneasiness she felt as each mile took her farther away from Lucas. There was absolutely no reason for it, she told herself irritably. Her mother had everything well in hand for the small reception, a ravishing dress hung in her wardrobe at the cottage; the result of an expedition to Knightsbridge with Ginny, and this time next week she would be on her honeymoon.

Doing her best to shake off her blues, Emily hugged her father when he met the train and chatted brightly to him on the drive back to the cottage, where she found her mother in the kitchen, making preparations for dinner.

'You look tired,' Claire Warner told her daughter. 'Sit there and watch, darling. Richard, you can make some tea, if you would.'

Emily did as she was told, enjoyed the meal later, and afterwards spent half an hour talking to Lucas on the phone. But once she was in bed, sent there early by her mother to get a good night's rest, she tossed and turned for most of it, her fey mood back in full force once she was alone.

For the next couple of days Emily tried hard to throw off her mood and show enthusiasm for the preparations, but halfway through the week, glad to escape for a while, she told her mother she had to make a swift trip to London for a few things she'd forgotten to pack for the honeymoon.

'Stay the night with Lucas, then,' said her practical mother. 'No point in wearing yourself out with two journeys.'

When Emily let herself into the familiar loft late that afternoon she realised, with a pang of disloyalty, that already it felt far more like home than her parents' cottage. In the master bedroom all was tidy, with Lucas's luggage standing by the bed, waiting to be packed. Emily took off her coat and kicked off her shoes. She would do something about a meal later. She let herself down on the bed, clutching Lucas's pillow to her chest, and surrendered to an overwhelming desire for sleep.

Emily woke reluctantly, fighting with whoever was trying to take the pillow away from her.

'Darling, wake up,' said Lucas, something in his voice cutting through the fog of sleep.

Emily sat up, smiling guiltily. 'I know I should have rung to tell you, but—'

'Never mind that.' He sat down beside her, his eyes searching as he took the hand wearing the ring they'd chosen together. 'Tell me what's wrong, Emily. Have you changed your mind?'

Now she was fully awake Emily saw that Lucas was as white as his shirt. 'About marrying you? Absolutely not!'

'Thank God for that,' he said, relaxing slightly. 'Forgive me for pointing out the obvious, darling, but you're not supposed to be here. Luckily, I rang the cottage before I left for home tonight, so I knew you'd made a sudden decision to come to London for the day.'

She nodded. 'There's something I have to tell you. Before the wedding, I mean.'

'You're worrying the hell out of me,' he said with sudden violence. 'For God's sake, tell me!'

'Sorry. It's just that I'm pregnant,' she said baldly.

'Pregnant?' Lucas stared at her blankly. '*How*? After what happened the first time I've taken every care not to put you at risk again.'

'I went to see Dr Hall on my way here today, Lucas; the one who came when you were ill. She said I'm six weeks pregnant.'

They gazed at each other in silence.

'So it happened that night, after all,' said Lucas slowly. 'But I thought—'

'So did I,' said Emily. 'The usual signs appeared, as I told you, but nothing like normal, which I put down to the shock of the fall. But I knew something was wrong. If you remember, I was very clingy when you left on Monday morning. I felt so off-colour I thought I was sickening for something. Then, after supper last night, I was beginning to pack for the honeymoon and found the pregnancy test I'd never used. When it showed positive I thought I'd better get someone to confirm it, so I made an appointment with Dr Hall and came on here to give you the news.'

Sudden comprehension dawned in Lucas's eyes, and he pulled her into his arms and held her cruelly tight in silence.

'Aren't you going to say anything?' said Emily after a while.

'I'm too busy thanking God you didn't find this out sooner,' he said hoarsely, and kissed her hard. 'Otherwise you wouldn't be marrying me on Saturday, would you? I'd just be a signature on some child-support agreement!'

She shook her head, burrowing closer. 'I can't imagine that, now.'

'Good.' He tipped her face up to his. 'Then you'd better bow to the inevitable, bride-to-be. The wedding's definitely on.'

'Alice would kill you, for a start, if she couldn't wear the hat,' agreed Emily unsteadily.

'If your brother hadn't already saved her the trouble!'

They collapsed on the bed together, half laughing, half not, and held each other close in silent thanksgiving for a while.

'I couldn't have done it, anyway, Lucas,' said Emily eventually.

He propped himself on an elbow to give her a searching look. 'Done what, exactly?'

'Kept to my obligation hang-ups.'

His eyes lit up. 'Thank God for that. But why not, darling?'

'Because I fell head over heels in love with you the

first moment I saw you.' She grinned. 'Red nose and hacking cough included.'

'And, ill though I was, I wanted to grab you off my kitchen stool and make love to you there and then,' said Lucas, inching nearer.

'Did you really?' she said, starry-eyed, then sighed heavily. 'But there's something else I ought to confess, too.'

'Oh, God,' he groaned. 'Go on. Tell me the worst.'

'I've based the hero of my novel on you. Do you mind?'

He fell flat on his back in relief. 'Not in the least—as long as he's tall, dark and amazingly handsome, and the story has a happy ending.'

'All of the above,' she assured him. 'In my fairy-tale, Cinderella will firmly ignore all half-baked principles and marry her prince. If he uses sufficient persuasion.'

Lucas rolled over to kiss her. 'I'm no prince, darling.'

'True. But you're *very* good at persuasion.' Emily wriggled closer. 'I could use some of it now. And I don't mean friendly persuasion, either.'

'Good. Because the red-hot passionate kind is the only thing on offer,' her bridegroom informed her.

'Bliss,' sighed Emily, and smiled up at him with such love in her eyes that Lucas closed his for an instant, then kissed her again.

'I know the happy ever after bit is supposed to start after the actual wedding,' he said huskily, 'but for me it began almost from the moment I surprised you in my kitchen, Cinderella.'

'Same for me,' she assured him happily. 'Thank goodness you went down with flu!'

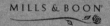

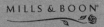

MILLS & BOON

Modern Romance™

NATHAN'S CHILD by Anne McAllister

When Nathan Wolfe discovers the only woman he
ever loved has hidden his child from him, his life
changes in a moment. Carin Campbell had good
reasons for keeping their child a secret – but now
Nathan is demanding they marry. Carin can't marry
him – she knows he's proposed out of duty, not love…

MOTHER AND MISTRESS by Kay Thorpe

Lauren is looking for her adopted daughter Kerry – not
a husband! But the moment she arrives at Brad
Laxton's mansion he makes his attraction to her very
clear. Becoming nanny to the daughter she was forced
to give up is hard enough – and now Lauren must resist
the charms of Kerry's adoptive father…

MIDNIGHT RHYTHMS by Karen van der Zee

The last thing Sam wants is a stranger in her house –
but David is always there. Making her angry, making
her laugh, giving her all the fun she's been missing – and
showing just how much he desires her… Sam doesn't
want to fall in love – but David's charms are breaking
down her defences…

THE BOSS'S URGENT PROPOSAL by Susan Meier

Olivia Brady had been head over heels in lust with her
boss, Josh Nicholson, for four years – but he had no
idea! She knew it was time to move on – and then Josh
demanded she stay. He realised he wanted her for
more than her organisational skills – but could he put
his doubts about love aside…?

On sale 2nd May 2003

*Available at most branches of WH Smith,
Tesco, Martins, Borders, Eason, Sainsbury's
and all good paperback bookshops.*

0403/01b

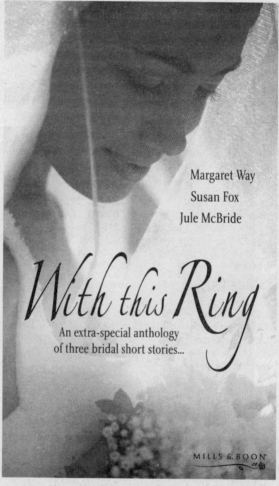

Margaret Way

Susan Fox

Jule McBride

With this Ring

An extra-special anthology
of three bridal short stories...

MILLS & BOON

Available from 18th April 2003

2 FREE

books and a surprise gift!

We would like to take this opportunity to thank you for reading this Mills & Boon® book by offering you the chance to take TWO more specially selected titles from the Modern Romance™ series absolutely FREE! We're also making this offer to introduce you to the benefits of the Reader Service™—

- ★ FREE home delivery
- ★ FREE gifts and competitions
- ★ FREE monthly Newsletter
- ★ Exclusive Reader Service discount
- ★ Books available before they're in the shops

Accepting these FREE books and gift places you under no obligation to buy, you may cancel at any time, even after receiving your free shipment. Simply complete your details below and return the entire page to the address below. *You don't even need a stamp!*

YES! Please send me 2 free Modern Romance books and a surprise gift. I understand that unless you hear from me, I will receive 4 superb new titles every month for just £2.60 each, postage and packing free. I am under no obligation to purchase any books and may cancel my subscription at any time. The free books and gift will be mine to keep in any case.

P3ZEA

Ms/Mrs/Miss/Mr ....Initials...................................

BLOCK CAPITALS PLEASE

Surname ....

Address ....

....

....Postcode................................

Send this whole page to:
UK: FREEPOST CN81, Croydon, CR9 3WZ
EIRE: PO Box 4546, Kilcock, County Kildare (stamp required)

Offer valid in UK and Eire only and not available to current Reader Service subscribers to this series. We reserve the right to refuse an application and applicants must be aged 18 years or over. Only one application per household. Terms and prices subject to change without notice. Offer expires 31st July 2003. As a result of this application, you may receive offers from Harlequin Mills & Boon and other carefully selected companies. If you would prefer not to share in this opportunity please write to The Data Manager at the address above.

Mills & Boon® is a registered trademark owned by Harlequin Mills & Boon Limited.
Modern Romance™ is being used as a trademark.